A Person of Interest

A Person of Interest

ERNEST HILL

KENSINGTON PUBLISHING CORP.
http://www.kensingtonbooks.com

DAFINA BOOKS are published by

Kensington Publishing Corp.
850 Third Avenue
New York, NY 10022

All Kensington titles, imprints and distributed lines are available at special quantity discounts for bulk purchases for sales promotion, premiums, fund-raising, educational or institutional use.

Special book excerpts or customized printings can also be created to fit specific needs. For details, write or phone the office of the Kensington Special Sales Manager: Kensington Publishing Corp., 850 Third Avenue, New York, NY 10022. Attn. Special Sales Department. Phone: 1-800-221-2647.

Dafina Books and the Dafina logo Reg. U.S. Pat. & TM Off.

ISBN 0-7582-1312-3

First Kensington Trade Paperback Printing: October 2006
10 9 8 7 6 5 4 3 2 1

Printed in the United States of America

In loving memory of my mother,
Katie Mae Hill.
October 12, 1931–February 10, 2006

A kind and gentle soul who lived her faith
and inspired us all.

She gave me love.
She gave me joy.
She gave me perfect right.
She gave me . . .

CHAPTER 1

The deafening sounds of the sirens fell silent, and through the partially opened blinds of my bedroom window, I could see the twirling beams of light casting long shadows on the house across the street. And though I was only partially conscious, there was in me an overbearing urge to rise, for I could not imagine, try as I may, what ungodly occurrence could have caused such upheaval in our quaint community at such an unseemly hour of the morning. And as I hastily draped a robe over my scantily clad body and a scarf over my freshly curled hair, I could hear rising from the streets the panicked sound of people scurrying about, and I could hear the muddled sound of a man's authoritative voice barking out a series of unintelligible orders, and could hear the screeching wail of a pained woman screaming at the top of her lungs.

And those sounds incited me again, and I pulled the sash tighter about my waist and slipped my bare feet into my old house slippers and made my way out of the house and into the darkness. And the sight of the yellow police tape strung around Luther's house confused me. As did the ambulance that was backed against his front porch, and the fire truck and three squad cars parked on the shoulder just beyond his front yard. And I was staring at the scene, trying to make some sense of things, when I heard her pained voice again.

And I saw that it was his wife's mother, and she was hanging onto a paramedic, and her limp legs were like spaghetti, and there was an awful smell in the air and I saw Luther standing before the porch with his hands clasped over his mouth and a police officer was standing next to him, and in the officer's hands was a pad. And as my eyes moved beyond his face and I inched closer to the yellow tape, I noticed that the front door of his house was open, and there was a trail of white smoke floating out of the house and billowing high into the early morning air. And until this moment, I had thought that this was simply a fire that had burned out of control, but now I sensed something more.

And I was struggling with those feelings and trying to make some sense of the chaos when I approached the yellow tape and noticed two policemen passing back and forth before the front door. The porch light was on, as were the lights inside the house, and I could see several other officers congregating at a spot just inside the door, and I opened my mouth to question the officer standing on the opposite side of the tape, but before I could summon the words, he spoke first.

"Move back," he said. "You can't go in there." And he looked at me with eyes made stern by the seriousness of the moment.

"What happened?" I asked.

"Move back," he said again. "Please move back."

I stepped back into the street, and though it was a warm, humid morning, I felt a chill sweep over me and I tugged at my robe and as I did, I saw another officer rush from the house and out toward the street. And when he was near the officer guarding the perimeter, he paused and spoke.

"There's gasoline all over the goddamn place," he said. Then I saw him look toward the cars parked along the street. "They here yet?"

"Over there," the other officer said.

I saw him squint and look. A third officer was struggling to remove a large dog from the rear of his car.

"Get that goddamn dog over here," he yelled.

I watched him for a moment, then I turned and looked at Luther, and I could see that he had collapsed to the ground, crying. And I could see his body trembling, and I could see his large, powerful hands pounding the ground, and I wanted to go to him, but I knew that I could not, and the fact that I could not pained me. And I was staring at Luther when I saw the officer gingerly lift him to his feet and escort him away from the house and out toward one of the squad cars parked just beyond the yard. And as they disappeared into the shadows I was aware of the foul odor again, and the people milling about the streets, and next to me, I heard Brother Jenkins say that Luther had just made it home, and that he had found his wife and son's smoldering bodies huddled together just inside the door, and they had been doused with gasoline, and they were burned beyond recognition, and that it was a goddamn shame for one person to do that to another person, and that when they caught the son of a bitch that did this, they ought to hang him upside down by his baby maker and beat him to death with horse wire.

And in the distance, I saw the car with Luther in it pull out into the street, and I heard the officer say that they were headed downtown to take his statement. And as they passed, I saw Luther slumped over in the front seat with his forearms folded against the dashboard and his head lying against his arms. And as I watched the car disappear into the curb, I felt my eyes moisten, and I wondered how Luther was going to go on without his family, and I wondered how Mrs. Miller was going to go on without her child. And on the horizon, I saw the light of the rising sun breaking through the darkness, illuminating the ugliness of this godforsaken day. And suddenly, I could not help but notice the stillness of the morning, or the way the huge branches of the old oak tree in the yard before Luther's house hung perfectly still in the warm, breezeless air. Or the spot beneath that tree where, from across the street in the window of my parents' house, I had recently watched him and her lying on a blanket laden with food, laughing and frolicking and making merry like it was Christmas. And I was looking at that spot, remembering them, when I heard the distant sound of my mother's feeble voice calling to me from the depths of her front porch.

CHAPTER 2

The door to my house was open, and from where I stood, I could see the tiny trail of smoke rising from their badly charred bodies. And I could smell the strong scent of their burning flesh. And the officer they called A.J. was standing next to me. And he was asking me questions and writing on his pad. And I could hear the commotion all about me. And my trembling hands were covering my mouth, and I could not move. And I could not breathe. And I could not stop the tears from streaming down my face. And through the chaos, I heard Chief Harlan Ladue's voice rising above the mayhem.

"A.J., get him out of here!" he screamed. "He don't need to see them like this!"

And I saw A.J. click his ink pen shut and place it in his shirt pocket. And when he did, I heard the chief call to him again.

"And tell Billy Ray to keep everybody behind that goddamn tape. I don't want to see anybody trampling over this crime scene. You hear?"

"Yes, sir, Chief," A.J. called back to him.

And then he eased next to me, and I felt him take my lifeless arm and place it about his neck. And his weight was supporting my weight. And I felt myself leaning hard against his body, and I felt my weak, wobbly legs keeping time with his as we proceeded to his car, which was parked on the road just beyond the house.

And as we walked, I noticed the neighbors standing on their stoops, many of them still wearing their nightclothes, and I saw others standing in the road that ran past my house, and they were all looking at me, and I knew that like me, they were trying to figure out what in the hell had happened.

When we reached the car, A.J. pulled the door open on the passenger's side and I slid onto the seat, and a second officer approached him, and I heard him tell the officer that he was taking me downtown, and that he would get my statement, and that this was one of the most brutal crimes that he had seen in Brownsville in his twenty-three years on the force. Then I heard him tell the officer to keep the crowd behind the tape because the chief didn't want anybody trampling over the crime scene. Then he climbed behind the wheel—the window on the passenger's side of the car was down and the other officer spoke to me. I could see his lips moving and I could hear him talking, but I could not focus.

So I turned my face away from the window, and I closed my eyes, and laid my head upon the dash. And I could feel the car moving out into the street, I could hear the people outside the car talking, and I could smell the scent of burning flesh, and I could feel the tears stinging my eyes. And I could feel the intense pain of my aching heart. I was in a nightmare, and darkness was all about. And the world was spinning, and all I wanted was to die.

I felt the car navigating the curb, and then I felt it accelerate, and I knew we were on the long stretch of highway leading downtown. And inside my tormented mind, I wished that this were a normal day. And I wished I was at work, and I wished Juanita was sitting at the kitchen table having her morning coffee, and I wished Darnell was still in bed, sleeping. And I wished that I had come home sooner, and I wished that none of this had happened.

We passed the old train depot, and my head was still bowed, and my mind was whirling, but in spite of it all, I could hear the townsfolk milling out near the street. And I was certain they had heard the sirens, that by now someone had given them the news, and like everybody else in town, they were speculating on what had happened, and on who in God's name would do such a thing.

And I had asked myself that question a thousand times and a thousand times I had drawn a blank. And I had prayed over and over again for this nightmare to end. But pray as I might, I knew that when I again raised my head and opened my eyes, the horror of this day would still be before me. And I wished that I could keep my head bowed and my eyes closed and that I could somehow stave off that terrible moment which, at present, I neither had the courage nor the desire to face.

At the station, A.J. pulled into the large parking lot behind the courthouse just off the square, and I followed him through the side door of the police station. Outside, the sun was just beginning to rise, and there were a few people milling about the square and one of the trustees was outside, washing a car, and I saw him looking at me, and I knew he was wondering if my presence had anything to do with the sirens. I saw him, and yet I did not see him. I was outside of myself, mindlessly following the officer while struggling to stand and struggling to put one foot in front of the other.

I followed him into the building, and he led me down a narrow hall to a small room which sported only a table and two chairs. When I entered the room, he motioned for me to sit down, which I did. Then he pulled the chair out as if he, too, was going to sit, but before he did, he hesitated and looked at me.

"Can I get you a cup of coffee?" he asked.

I looked at him, but I didn't answer. I couldn't. I saw him look at the officer standing just beyond the door.

"Get him a cup of coffee," he said.

I saw him remove an empty cup, fill it with coffee, then hand it to me. I raised the cup to my mouth but my hands were shaking so badly, I only managed to take a sip before I had to set the cup down. I was dead inside—my nerves were shot, and I could not stop trembling. I saw A.J. sit down directly across from me. He took the pad and pencil from his pocket, and after he had flipped through the pad a moment, he looked up at me.

"Mr. Jackson," he said in a low, sympathetic voice.

"Yes, sir," I said, and I could feel my voice breaking.

He paused again, and I saw him study the pad. "I'm sorry to

have to put you through this again," he said, "but I'm afraid we
need to go over this one more time. Can you do that?"

"I'll try," I said.

I saw him look at the pad again, then click on the tape
recorder.

"Let's see," he said. "I believe you said you discovered the bodies at approximately five A.M. Is that correct?"

"Yes, sir," I said.

And through the dazed state which was now my reality, I heard
myself sobbing. And I closed my eyes and buried my face in my
hands. And I could see the image of their smoldering bodies lying
before the door. And I could smell the stench of their burning
flesh. And I only wished that I could die.

CHAPTER 3

I turned and looked back toward the house. I could see that Mama had come out onto the porch, and she was still wearing the long, white nightgown that she had worn to bed the night before and from where I stood, I could see her looking at me and I knew she was wondering what was going on. So, I made my way back across the street and up the steps leading onto the porch. My nerves were frazzled, my head was spinning, and I wanted to sit down, but there was only one chair on the porch and I left it vacant just in case Mama wanted to sit.

"What's all the commotion about?" Mama asked.

I saw her brace herself against the old deep-freezer, and I wished that she would sit down. Mama had grown old. She was nearly seventy-five—and her heart was impaired and her pressure was high, and she was suffering with rheumatoid arthritis.

"Was there a fire?" she asked. "I see the fire truck over there. Did Luther's house catch on fire?"

"No, ma'am," I said. Suddenly, I could feel my body trembling.

"They're dead," I said.

"Who?"she asked.

"Luther's wife and son," I said. My voice broke and I felt like crying.

"Dead!"

"Yes, ma'am," I said. "Somebody killed them."

"My God!" I heard Mama gasp. "Who would do such a thing?"

Mama had been standing against the wall, but now she walked closer to the screen and I saw her looking across at Luther's house. The police were still there, and now it all made sense to her. The yellow tape, the fire truck, the ambulance, the police. She looked for a moment, then she spoke again.

"Where Luther?"

"They took him downtown," I said.

I saw her look at the house again. Then back at me.

"For what?" she said.

"They say he found the bodies," I said.

Suddenly, her eyes grew wide.

"They don't think he had nothing to do with this, do they?"

"No, ma'am," I said. "I'm sure they just want to ask him a few questions."

Across the street I saw the policeman open the door on Luther's old truck and the dog jumped inside; then the officer waved the chief over, and the two of them walked around the truck—and I saw the chief smile and pat the officer on the shoulder and I saw the officer bend down and hug the dog hard. And I was watching him and wondering what was going on, when I heard Mama's frail voice say, "Look like we got company." I looked toward the street and saw T-Baby, the only black officer on the Brownsville police force, walking toward our porch.

"Morning," he said.

"Morning, T-Baby," I said.

I saw him frown and look at me strangely—I knew he was trying to figure out who I was.

"Felicia," he said. "Is that you?"

"It's me," I said.

I saw him smile, then slap his knee with his hand.

"Well, I'll be," he said. "Last I heard you were married and living somewhere out in California."

"Los Angeles," I said.

I saw him tilt his head and look past me.

"Your husband come with you?"

"No," I said. "He died about three months ago. Liver cancer."

"Oh, I'm sorry to hear that," he said. "If there's anything I can do for you, just let me know. You hear?"

"Thank you," I said. "I will."

I saw him remove his hat and wipe his forehead with the back of his hand. Then he looked across the street, then back at me.

"Well," he said, "we got ourselves a pretty bad situation over there. Two people dead and no real clues as to why." He paused and looked at me again. "Were you home last night?"

"I was here," I said.

"Did you happen to see or hear anything suspicious?"

"Over there?" I asked, looking toward Luther's house.

"Yes, ma'am," he said.

"No, I didn't."

"Did your parents?"

I looked at Mama. She shook her head.

"Well, did you notice any strangers or any strange vehicles in the neighborhood?"

"No," I said.

I saw T-Baby sigh, then scratch his head. "Well, do you know if they were having any kind of trouble?"

"Who?" I asked.

"Luther," he said. "And his wife."

"Luther!" I said. "You don't suspect Luther, do you?"

"Right now we don't have any suspects," he said. "Just two dead people and a husband who was gone all night."

"T-Baby," I said, "you know Luther wouldn't do anything like that in a million years. You know that as well as I do."

"I'm not saying that he did."

"They were good family people," Mama said. "They seem to get along nicely. And Luther was crazy about that boy. Now, I don't know what happened, but I don't believe he would hurt that child."

I saw T-Baby take a handkerchief from his pocket and mop the sweat from his face. Then he looked at me. And suddenly his eyes grew serious.

"When was the last time you spoke to Luther?"

"It's been years," I said.

I saw him studying my face, and I knew why he had asked me. We were all the same age, T-Baby, Luther, and me. And we had all gone to high school together. I had been in love with Luther, and Luther had been in love with me. And I had wanted the two of us to spend our lives together. But Luther's mother died, and he started seeing Juanita, and I moved away and married another man, and not just another man, but a man of means. And even after I had gotten married, I still longed to see Luther again. But he refused, and instead he married Juanita and they had a child. I was never the same. And everybody around here knew that. And now, I was back, and this had happened. And that's why T-Baby asked. Because he knew that I had loved Luther, and Luther had loved me.

"Have you ever known Luther to be violent?" he asked.

"Never," I said.

Mama had been leaning against the deep-freezer, but now she pushed away and stood upright.

"Why you asking all these question about Luther?" she asked.

"Just doing my job," he said.

"He didn't have anything to do with this," I said.

"Well, I hope you're right," T-Baby said. "But as it stands, he's the last known person to have seen them alive."

"So he is a suspect," I said.

"No," T-Baby said. "Not a suspect. A person of interest."

CHAPTER 4

I raised my head and tried to compose myself. I could hear the sound of the tape spinning in the tiny tape recorder that A.J. had placed in the center of the table. I wanted to stop crying and answer his questions and do all that I could to help him find the killer, but there was a throbbing pain where my heart was and my mind was whirling and I could not focus. I saw A.J. look at the pad again, then scratch his head.

"You said you left your house shortly before ten P.M. last night. Is that correct?"

"Yes, sir," I said.

"And you returned shortly before five this morning?"

"Yes, sir."

"Where did you go?" he asked me.

"I just drove around."

He looked up and for the first time, I looked into his greyish-blue eyes and I could see that my answer had puzzled him.

"Was it customary for you to stay away from home all night?"

"No, sir," I said.

He paused and I could tell he wanted me to explain.

"We had an argument," I said.

"You and your wife?"

"Yes, sir."

"So you two were having problems?"

"No more than any other married folks."

"Did you argue or did you fight?"

"We argued," I said.

He paused again and scribbled on the pad.

"What was the first thing you did when you returned home?"

"I went inside."

"Was the door locked?"

"No, sir. It wasn't."

"Did you lock it before you left?"

"I don't know," I said. "I left in such a hurry. I just don't know."

"What exactly did you see when you entered the house?"

"I saw the bodies."

"So the lights were on when you returned."

"Yes, sir," I said. "They were on."

"Were they on when you left?"

"Yes, sir," I said.

"And that was around ten?"

"Yes, sir."

"What did you do when you saw the bodies?"

"I didn't know what to do," I said. Then I paused, crying.

"But you did do something."

"Yes, sir," I said.

"What?"

"I called 911. Then I called Juanita's mother."

"Did you touch the bodies before you made the calls?"

"Yes, sir," I said.

"Did you move them?"

"No, sir," I said. "I shook them."

"You shook them?"

"Yes, sir," I said. I paused again. I could feel my bottom lip quivering. "I shook them to see if they were dead."

"But you didn't move them?"

"No, sir," I said. "I didn't."

"Did you go into any other room of the house?"

"No, sir."

"Did you go outside?"

"No, sir."

"What time does your wife normally go to bed?"

"Ten," I said. "Sometimes a little later."

"And what time did you say you left again?"

"Ten," I said.

He paused again and thumbed through the tablet.

"Did anybody see you leave?"

"No, sir," I said. "Not that I know of."

"Did you talk to anybody?"

"No, sir," I said. "I didn't."

"When you left," he said, "where did you go?"

"I just drove around."

"All night?"

"No, sir," I said. "Just for an hour or two."

"And after that?"

"I went to the hotel over in Cedar Lake."

"What time did you check in?"

"I didn't."

"You went to the hotel but you didn't check in?"

"Yes, sir," I said. "That's correct."

"Why not?" he said.

"I didn't have any money."

"So you left?"

"No, sir," I said. "I parked in the parking lot."

"So, you slept in your car?"

"Yes, sir."

"What time did you leave?"

"Around a quarter 'til five."

"A quarter until five."

"Yes, sir," I said. "I had to be at work at six. So, I tried to give myself at least an hour to take a bath and get ready."

"Where do you work?"

"I work for Louisiana Machinery."

"Doing what?"

"I work on big Cats."

"Excuse me?"

"I repair heavy equipment."

"You're a mechanic?"

"Yes, sir," I said.

"Did you talk to anybody at the hotel before you left?"

"No, sir," I said. "I didn't."

"So no one saw you from the time you left home at ten until you returned home the next day at five."

"No, sir," I said. "They didn't."

"When you made it home, did you see anything suspicious?"

"No, sir," I said.

"Was anything missing?"

"I don't know."

"Did you check?"

"No, sir. I didn't. I just called 911."

"And after you made the call, what did you do?"

"Nothing," I said.

"Your wife and kid lying on the floor dead and you didn't do anything?"

"I didn't know what to do."

"Did you look around to see if the killer was still in the house?"

"No, sir," I said.

"Did you try to see how the killer had gotten in?"

"No, sir," I said.

"Why not?"

"I don't know."

"Don't you find it kind of strange that the killer would take the time to burn the bodies before he left?"

"No, sir," I said. "Not really."

"Well, how did he know you wasn't coming back?"

"I don't know," I said.

"Didn't you say that it was abnormal for you to be away all night?"

"Yes, sir," I said.

"Then why would he take such a chance?"

"I don't know why," I said.

"I'll tell you one possibility," he said. "Perhaps he knew he had all night."

I remained quiet.

"Did you kill your family?" he asked.

"No, sir, " I said. "I loved my family."

CHAPTER 5

T-Baby asked a few more questions and when he was con-vinced that I had told him all that I knew, he departed our yard and joined the two officers who previously had been inside Luther's house but were now standing in Luther's yard just be-yond the front porch. And though he neither looked nor gestured in my direction, I knew he was recounting what I had just told him. And the fact that he was trying to use my words to pin this on Luther angered me. For as long as I could recall, I had never known Luther to exhibit any behavior that would vaguely suggest he'd be capable of such a heinous crime. To the contrary, he had always been a kind and gentle man who possessed the spirit of a thousand angels. I knew that, and T-Baby knew that, and for him to suggest otherwise was inexcusable.

I needed to see Luther. I needed to look deep into his eyes and see for myself that he was, in fact, who he had always been. Yes, I would go to him and I would sit on one side of the table and he on the other, and at that moment, I will not concern myself with what some people might think or with what other people might say. I will only concern myself with his large, beautiful eyes, for in those eyes I will see the truth of this thing as it really existed and not as others would have me believe. Long ago, when I was his and he was mine, it was always those beautiful brown eyes which were set perfectly into his handsome brown face that calmed me and told me where I stood with him and where he stood with me.

I had just decided to go to him when I was again aware of the sound of my mother's voice, and in that instant, I turned and looked at her. From the expression on her face, I was convinced that this had not been her first attempt to draw me back from the distant place to which my mind had drifted, and as I stood staring absently at her, I heard her say that all of this was too much for her to digest and that her pressure was up and she was going to go back inside and lay down for a little while. And I started to follow her, but before I could, I saw Miss Olivia making her way across the street. She was wearing a long housecoat and leaning heavily on her walking cane and I could tell by the look in her old jaundiced eyes—she was seventy-three years old and had lived in the neighborhood longer than everyone except Mama—that she had been badly shaken by the murder that had occurred in the house adjacent to hers.

Behind me, I heard Mother's bedroom door open and close, and I heard the bedspring creak, and I saw the light from her bedroom window fade to darkness. And in that instant, I turned back toward the old screen door and watched patiently as Miss Olivia pulled her feeble body up the steps leading onto the porch. And as I watched her, I hoped that this terrible tragedy which had befallen our peaceful little community had not so unnerved her that she or, for that matter, the smattering of others in the neighborhood like her would be unable to feel either safe or secure in the most sacred place on earth for people of their ilk—their homes.

I held the screen door open for her and I felt the tight grip of her unsteady hand clutching my arm, and as she mounted the porch, I could tell that crossing the street and climbing the steps had taken a great deal out of her.

"Take your time," I cautioned her. But she neither spoke nor looked at me. Instead, she concentrated on the steps, gingerly navigating one after the other until she was securely on the porch.

And as I guided her to the vacant chair, I secretly wished that she had not come, for at this very moment I longed to be in the privacy of my bedroom, preparing to go to the man that I had once loved more than life itself. And as she eased onto the seat, I briefly glanced across the street. In the distance I could see that T-Baby had lowered himself to his hands and knees and was looking underneath Luther's front porch. And suddenly, we were all young again and I was still his, and he was still mine, and our lives were before us and I was lying in his arms, on a blanket, in the park, beneath a wild-oak tree. We had just made love—and he was mine and I was his, and we swore that we would be together forever until death did us part. And I was reveling in that moment when I again heard the feeble sound of Miss Olivia's voice.

"I never thought I'd live to see something like this," she said. And as she spoke she slowly shook her head from one side to the other. "Not around here. And not in my own backyard."

"No, ma'am," I said. "Neither did I."

After that, it was quiet again. She sat facing the screen and I stood just behind her, leaning against the freezer. I could see that she was staring at Luther's house and, like the rest of us, she had been awakened by the sound of the sirens. Her straight white hair was still neatly tied beneath a satin head scarf and the hem of her coarse white nightgown hung just below the bottom of her tattered brown housecoat.

"I saw you talking to T-Baby," she said, still looking across the street. "Did he tell you anything?"

"No, ma'am," I said. "He didn't."

Suddenly, she turned her head and looked directly at me and I could see her hands shaking. She lived alone, and the killings had happened just beyond her yard. I figured she was thinking it could have just as easily been her. There was no reason to think that way, but I could tell that she was. As she looked at me, she did not speak, and I sensed that she was waiting for me to say more, but when I did not, she spoke again.

"You reckon he did it?" she asked.

"No, ma'am," I said. "I don't."

My mind drifted again. And I wondered where they had taken Luther, and if he was all right, and whether they had charged him.

"Well, they were having problems," she said.

"What kind of problems?"

"I don't know, exactly," she said. "But I did hear them arguing."

I had been standing by the freezer, but now I moved closer to her.

"Recently?" I asked.

"Last night."

"Did you tell the police?"

"I told them."

"And what did they say?"

"Nothing."

"Nothing?" I said. "Are you sure?"

"Well, the heavyset one did say that they were going to look into it. And then he asked me if I had seen Luther leave the house last night. I told him I had, and he asked me about what time and I told him around ten or eleven. I didn't know exactly."

"Could you tell what they were fighting about?"

"No, I couldn't. But from the way it sounded, it was serious."

"What do you mean?"

"Yelling and screaming and such."

"Well, all married folks argue," I said.

"They weren't just arguing," she said. "They were fighting." She paused again, and I saw her look toward Luther's house again. "I just hope that boy didn't up and do something that he's gone live to regret."

"No," I said. "Luther wouldn't do that."

"I pray to God you're right," she said. "But somebody did it, and I don't think I'll be able to rest again until they catch him."

"Well, you're welcome to stay with us until this is resolved."

"No, I think I'll call my sister over in Jackson and see if she'll come stay with me awhile."

"Well, if she can't, the offer still stands."

"I appreciate that," Miss Olivia said. "But if she can't come here,

I'll go there. I don't think I'll feel safe anyway until they catch the person who did this."

Across the street, the coroner arrived, and we watched quietly as they bagged the bodies and removed them from the house. And when they were done, she rose to her feet.

"Well, I guess I'll try to make it on home."

"Would you like some coffee before you go?"

"No, thank you," she said. "I got a pot on the stove."

CHAPTER 6

After I said that, A.J. looked at me for a long time and I figured he was trying to determine if I was telling him the truth or not. When we had first begun to talk, he had seemed cordial enough, but now his demeanor had changed and he seemed agitated with me and perturbed by the answers I was giving him. I diverted my eyes for a moment and when I looked back, I saw him flipping through the pad again and in my mind, I assumed he was weighing his next question.

"I noticed a lawn mower underneath your porch," he said in a calm, steady voice. "Do you mow your own lawn?"

"Yes, sir," I said. "Either me or my boy."

He paused and leaned back in his chair.

"Do you mow it every week?"

"Yes, sir," I said. "Every Friday."

"Who mowed it last?"

"I did," I said.

He frowned and his gaze intensified.

"Are you sure?"

"I'm sure," I said. "Darnell was supposed to mow it but he had a game."

"Darnell is your son?"

"Yes, sir," I said.

He looked at me, and I could see that he was perplexed by

something that I had said. He looked down at the pad for a moment and then at me.

"Where's your gas can?"

"Sir?" I said, a little confused by his questions.

"We couldn't find your gas can."

"I don't know," I said.

"When was the last time you saw it?"

"I don't know."

"You mow your lawn every week and you don't remember the last time you saw your gas can?"

"No, sir," I said. "I don't."

"Where do you normally keep it?"

"Next to the mower," I said. "Underneath the house."

"It's not there," he said. "We checked."

He paused again. I remained quiet.

"Perhaps you took it with you when you left last night."

"No, sir," I said. "I didn't."

"And perhaps you discarded it somewhere between here and Cedar Lake," he said accusingly.

"No, sir," I said, shaking my head vociferously.

"Did you kill your wife?"

"No, sir," I said. "I didn't."

"But you did argue with her?"

"Yes, sir," I said. "I did."

"And a short time after you two argued, she wound up dead."

"Yes, sir," I said. "I guess so."

"What were you two arguing about?"

"It was nothing," I said.

"It must have been something," he said, "for you to stay out all night."

He looked at me, but I remained silent.

"Was she running around on you?"

"No, sir," I said. "She thought I was running around on her."

"Were you?"

"No, sir," I said. "I wasn't."

"Then why did she suspect you?"

"She said somebody told her that I was."

"Who?"

"I don't know."

"She didn't tell you?"

"No, sir," I said. "She didn't."

"Didn't you ask her?"

"Yes, sir, I asked her."

"And what did she say?"

"Just that someone had called her."

"Did she know the caller?"

"No, sir, she didn't. Whoever called didn't identify themselves."

"Was the caller male or female?"

"Female."

"And she didn't recognize the voice?"

"No, sir," I said. "She didn't."

"Do you have any idea who it might have been?"

"We were having problems," I said. "A lot of people knew that. It could have been anyone."

"Could it have been one of your old girlfriends?"

"I don't have an old girlfriend," I said.

"You don't?"

"No, sir," I said. "I don't."

He paused and wrote something on the pad, and when he was done he looked up again.

"Did your wife work?"

"Yes, sir," I said.

"Where?"

"At the high school,"

His eyes narrowed and he looked at me strangely.

"She was a teacher?"

"Yes, sir," I said. "She was."

"What did she teach?"

"English."

"How long had she been a teacher?"

"Nearly twenty years."

"Was she having any problems at work?"

"No, sir," I said. "At least, not that I know of."

Suddenly, the door opened and the chief and two officers entered the room. They both approached the table, but neither one of them sat. The chief had been wearing his hat, but he removed it and placed it on the table next to the recorder. He let out a deep sigh, then ran his fingers through his hair, and as he did, I looked up at him. He was a big man, well over six feet tall. He wasn't fat, but he did have a relatively large stomach, and I would guess that he was in his late fifties or early sixties. I had seen him from a distance many times, but this was the first time, other than the brief encounter at my house, that I had ever seen him face-to-face.

"Chief." A.J. spoke to him.

The chief nodded politely, then spoke to me.

"Mr. Jackson," he said with a slight nod. In response, I nodded back. Out of the corner of my eye, I saw A.J. push away from the table as if he were about to stand, but before he could, the chief told him to keep his seat. After A.J. had repositioned his chair next to the table, the chief's eyes settled on me.

"My condolences again for your loss," the chief said. "I know this is hard on you, but I assure you we will do everything we can to get to the bottom of this."

"Yes, sir," I said, and I could feel my eyes begin to water again.

"Do you need anything?" the chief asked me. "Water? A soda? More coffee?"

"No, sir," I said, wiping my eyes with the back of my hand.

"Well, do you need to call anybody?"

"No, sir," I said. "Not right now."

The chief paused and removed a white handkerchief from his shirt pocket. He wiped the sweat from his forehead and then from the back of his neck. It was already seventy-five degrees outside and not much cooler in the small, windowless interrogation room in which we sat. After the chief had returned the handkerchief to his pocket, he resumed his questions.

"Mr. Jackson," he said, "do you know of anyone who would want to harm your wife and child?"

"No, sir," I said. "I don't."

"No one at all?"

"No, sir," I said. "No one."

"Well," he said, "she definitely knew her killer."

I felt my eyes watering again, and I found myself looking beyond them at the bare concrete wall, and suddenly I wasn't there anymore—I was with her and we were in the little sitting room just off the kitchen. And I had told her that she need not worry anymore, because I would take extra work and help catch everything up, and when I had, she would be able to relax. And she wouldn't have to cry anymore, and we could be a family again, just like we had been before we got so behind on our bills. I was thinking about that when I heard the chief's voice again.

"Does anyone else have a key to your house?"

"No, sir," I said.

"Do you have any idea who would have stopped by your house at such a late hour?" the chief asked me.

"No, sir," I said. "I don't."

"Well," the chief said with a deep sigh, "she either opened the door and let the killer in or the killer let himself in, because there's no sign of forced entry."

I looked at him, but I didn't say anything. I couldn't.

"A.J., what do you think?" the chief asked. I saw A.J. place his pencil on the table and look up from the pad.

"Well, Chief," he began, "she definitely knew her killer." A.J. shook his head. "And it doesn't appear to be a robbery. Mrs. Jackson's purse was sitting on the counter in plain view. And nothing was missing. We checked. Her wallet was still there, and it was full of money."

A.J. paused and looked at me. So did the chief. I didn't say anything, but I could feel the tears streaming down my face.

"And Chief," A.J. said, as though he had just remembered an

important detail, "it appears that Mrs. Jackson was killed first, and her son was apparently killed while he was still asleep. It appears that he was killed in his bedroom and moved to the living room. It just doesn't make sense, Chief. There doesn't appear to be a motive, but from the look of things whoever did this is a cold-hearted son of a bitch."

When he said that, he looked at me. I could feel my hands shaking and my lips quivering. I closed my eyes and buried my face in my hands and sobbed.

CHAPTER 7

Olivia left, and I went into the bathroom and began drawing my bath water. As I undressed, I could hear my mother beyond the wall that separated us, and I knew that like all of the others in the neighborhood, neither she nor I would be able to rest until more was learned about what had actually occurred across the street. And like the others, I also knew that any relevant news would be slow in coming. Though my mind told me to go on with my day as planned, I knew that I would not be able to concentrate on anything until I had heard something for myself. So, in spite of all I had to do, I decided to stay put until I had heard something definitive.

I removed my robe and hung it on the rack behind the door, and when I was done undressing, I eased into the water, and as I did, I looked around the bathroom. It had been years since I had actually lived with my parents, but very little about the bathroom had changed. There were four short walls, each bare except for a nondescript, tiny towel rack and a small wooden plaque inscribed with the Lord's Prayer. The large white tub was positioned on the longest wall, and high above the tub was a small window that looked out over the yard on the west side of the house.

Covering the window was an inexpensive curtain. The curtain was drawn, and the window was raised; I could hear the voices of a small group of men who had gathered at the house next door. I heard one of them say he had heard that Luther's old lady had caught him in bed with another man. And that she had threatened to expose him and that was the reason he killed her. I heard another one say that Luther had gotten behind on his house payments, and the bank was going to put him out, so he had killed his family for the insurance money. And I heard yet another one say he had heard that Luther had taken to drinking, and that he came home drunk last night. And his old lady had gotten mad, and then, he got mad and the liquor took over and he killed her.

As I listened to them, I remembered all too well why as a child I had hated this place so, and why I had longed to leave, and why until two weeks ago, after my husband died and my mother became ill, I had vowed to never come back. Yes, as I listened it all came back.

I remembered hating the way the houses were set so close to each other, and the way the streets twisted and turned from one block to the next, and the way the cemetery was situated at the far end of the community, reminding us that there was no way out of this godforsaken place, not even through death. And I remembered hating the fact that my father was a plumber, and that he was in business for himself, and that he felt obligated to the undesirables from the neighborhood. And I hated the way they hung around our house, begging him for work, and how they called at all hours of the night complaining about leaky faucets and busted pipes. And I hated how Daddy would leave his comfortable bed and crawl underneath their nasty houses, and how when he was finished, they were always too bad off to pay him. And I hated the way those same people talked about Daddy behind his back, and I hated the way they looked at Mama when Daddy's back was turned. And I hated the way they dragged around on the job, and I hated the way Mama cried because of all that Daddy had to deal with, and I hated the way those old busybodies gathered so close to our house to drink and gossip about that which they did not understand.

Somewhere along the street someone was brewing coffee. I

could smell the strong aroma riding on the warm morning breeze, and I wondered if they, too, like the men next door, were sitting around the breakfast table speculating about what had happened at Luther's house. As I wondered about them, my mind shifted to Luther, and I found myself once again worrying about him. Outwardly, he appeared to be a strong man. But I had known him intimately, and because I had, I knew that he was a gentle soul with the sensibilities of one who had been raised in a different place, and at a different time. And because I knew, it pained me to think of him once again attempting to cope with the loss of someone he loved. And I wanted to go to him and help him through this, but I knew that I could not. His wife and child had just died, and I was his old love, and this was a small town, and no one would understand—no one, not even my own mother.

So, like all of the others, I had but to wait for some semblance of news, and as I waited, I would pray to my God in heaven that this thing would pass quickly, and that they would find the monster who did this, and that in time, Luther would be able to stand again, and live again, and love again. And I was in the midst of my prayer when I heard my mother calling to me again. I stepped from the tub and draped my robe about my body, and when I was near Mother's room, I stopped and looked inside. She was sitting upright in her bed; her eyes were glassy, and her frail face seemed pale, and I feared at that moment that this had all been too much for her. And that fear caused me to rush to her side, and when I was next to her, I took her hand, and it was cold to the touch, and the coldness and rigidity of her skin caused an anxiety in me I heretofore had never known. And there was a feeling in me that she, too, was slipping away. Yes, I had seen this before in another place in my all-not-too-distant past when I had sat on the board of directors of an exclusive retirement community, and during a routine meeting I had seen an elderly associate succumb to a stroke and die. And at the moment of her demise, her eyes and her skin were as my mother's now appeared. And my knowledge of that moment caused a temporary paralysis in me. And I stood, as if outside my body, as my mother clutched her chest and pointed to the top drawer of her dresser.

"My medicine," she said.

I retrieved the small bottle of pills and removed the cap and handed them to her. There was a glass of water on the nightstand next to her bed. I passed it to her, and when I did, she placed the pills in her mouth and took two long gulps of water and then eased back onto her pillow, and I could see that she was in pain.

"Are you all right, Mother?" I asked.

"I just need to rest," she said.

"Can I do anything for you?"

"No," she said. "I'll be all right. After I rest a while."

She closed her eyes, and through the partially closed window, I could hear the murmur of the men's voices. I was sure that she could hear them, too, and I decided to go outside to ask them to hold it down a bit. I walked around the corner of the porch and stopped at the little wire-linked fence separating my mother's property from theirs. There were four of them sitting on the porch. Mr. Jim and Little Boy were sitting on the floor with their feet dangling just above the ground. Tae-Tae was sitting on the top step, and Monkey Biz was standing with his back against one of the posts. He was facing the road, but he was looking at Luther's house. And although it was early, they were already drinking. I could see three empty beer bottles on the floor. Monkey Biz was still holding his. I looked at the bottles, then back at them, re-pulsed.

"Could you men keep it down a little?" I said. "Mother's trying to rest. She's not feeling well."

"Sure thing, Miss Felicia," one of them said. "We didn't realize we were keeping up that much racket. Last thing we want to do is disturb Miss Hattie. That's the last thing in the world any of us want to do." He paused and looked at me sort of serious-like. "Ain't nothing seriously wrong, is it? With your mother, I mean. If you don't mind me asking."

"She's just a little under the weather," I said, not wanting to engage them in conversation. "She'll be fine once she gets a little rest."

"Well, if there's anything any of us can do."

"Just keep it down," I said.

"Yes, ma'am," he said. "Will do."

I turned to leave and as I did, I could feel their eyes on me, and I knew that they were watching me walk, and the fact that they were angered me. I started to turn and say something, but before I could, I heard one of them say, "That's one fine woman." And I heard another one say, "I don't know how Luther let that get away." The mentioning of his name caused me to look across the street, and I could see that the long strand of yellow tape was still strung around his yard, and I wondered where he was and what he was doing.

CHAPTER 8

The chief lit a cigarette, and I watched him and A.J. move away from the table and when they were positioned in the far corner, they began to speak in whispered tones, and every now and then, one of them would look at me and shake his head. And I had a strange feeling that they thought I had something to do with this, but as it stood, the evidence they had was shaky and they needed more time to flesh out the details. It seemed they had agreed upon that point and were about to dismiss me when the door leading into the small room swung open and my aunt walked in.

And when she did, the chief and A.J. said something to her, and as she started toward the table. I could see that she was disheveled and I could tell that she had been crying. And suddenly, I stood and we embraced each other, and I laid my head gently upon her bosom, and I felt the strength of her arms encircling me, and I cried as I never recalled crying before—and it was as if darkness was all about me and she was all I had to hold onto. And as I latched onto her with all of my strength, I felt her hand in the center of my back and I heard her say that she was sorry, and at that moment, I was neither conscious of the chief nor A.J. Instead, I was far from this place, lost in a terrible nightmare from which I could not awake. And death was all about me, and my wife was screaming, and my child was crying, and I was on an island looking at them from afar. And instinctively I knew that I would never live again. And I prayed, long and hard, for the swift moment of finality to sweep down from the heavens and usher me to that distant place of peace, for I knew that never again upon this earth would peace or happiness abide in me. And in the spirit of that realization, I wept with my head upon my aunt's bosom until I once again found myself listening to the sound of the chief's voice telling her that we were free to go. And as I walked aimlessly from the building, leaning heavily upon her for support, I was again aware of the drabness of the humid July morning and the coldness of this horrid world, which in one fleeting moment had taken from me all that gave my life meaning. And as we slowly navigated the desolate road to my aunt's tiny house far out in the country, she prayed, unceasingly, that almighty God would take me in his arms and hold and comfort me until this terrible nightmare had passed.

And as I listened to her, I fell into a deep stupor. And my mind and my soul surrendered all authority to the hurt and pain that was now my reality. And from that moment on, I secretly vowed neither to want nor desire anything again. And with that vow, I retreated deep within myself, and I closed the doors to a life that I no longer cared to live, and my aunt stood between me and the world from which I had retreated, and she took control of my affairs. And at her house, I slept for three long days. And when I again awakened and rejoined the living, I found myself sitting on the back seat of a long black limousine next to my aunt and across from my wife's mother and father. After the funeral procession slowly wound its way down one street after another, it was finally on the narrow, two-lane highway leading to the little red church where it had fallen upon Reverend Thomas to eulogize my wife and child. Though I had promised myself that I would hold firm, the sight of the little church caused my eyes to water and my knees to shake, and no sooner had the quivering begun when I felt my aunt's hand on my knee. And at that moment, I was glad that she was there, and I looked at her, but she did not look at me. Instead, she held her head erect, staring straight ahead, as if to say that her strength would be my strength, and this burden, no matter how difficult, was not mine to bear alone. And as the limo pulled onto the church grounds, I absorbed her strength and I told myself that I could do this. And I could do it because my aunt was here with me and because her strength would be my strength. And I kept telling myself that as I walked into the building and made my way down the narrow aisle and sat in the front pew only a few feet from the two flower-draped coffins containing the final remains of my beloved wife and child. And though my wife's mother and father had been in the limo with my aunt and me, her father had been extremely quiet and when he did speak, it had been to console his wife, who could not stop crying. I had wanted to say something to her as well, but there was nothing I could say, for I knew that she was blaming me.

She had not said it; neither had her husband, but I could tell on the few occasions that they had cause to look at me, that it was true. And because I knew that they felt as they did, I found it nearly impossible to look either of them in the eye. No, I had not killed my wife and child, but it was my fault that they were dead. I knew it, they knew it, and so did everyone else. For it was I who had argued with my wife that night, and it was I who had left my family alone, and it was I who had stood in this very church during our matrimonial moment and promised to cherish and protect her, and because I had failed to keep that promise, the unthinkable had happened. And as a result of my ineptitude, this sanctuary that had once marked our beginning, now marked our end, and the same family and friends who had come to witness our union were now present to pay their last respects, and I could feel their sad eyes on the back of my neck. And the grief and pain and angst of the town was heaped not simply upon the killer, but also upon me, which magnified the guilt that I already felt. And I wished that I were the one lying on display before the congregation instead of my wife and child.

And in the midst of my thoughts, the choir began to sing, and the sorrowful sound of their voices touched something deep within me. And the emotions which I had vowed to suppress burst forward and I buried my head in my hands, and as I cried, I felt my aunt's hands on me again, and I tried to draw from her strength, but at that moment, I realized that which I had already known: I was weak where she was strong. And the silent acknowledgment of that reality gave sanction to my emotions, and I mourned from a place so racked with pain that I felt I would never again be able to control my emotions and as I sobbed, I heard the deep, melodic tones of the church organ, and I heard the pained wail of my wife's mother, and I heard the prayerful voice of one of the elders say, "Help them, Jesus," and I felt my aunt's hand on me again, and I heard her calm, steady voice say: "It's going to be all right, child." And when the singing stopped, I kept my head bowed upon my lap and I could hear the moans throughout the church. One person after another made their way to the podium to talk about my wife and my child, and what their lives had meant to them, and how they were in heaven now, and how the pain and suffering of this old world was nevermore, and when they were done, the choir rose again and sang again, and my head was down. And I was still crying.

CHAPTER 9

I was sitting in the back of the church when Luther and his aunt entered. He was wearing a charcoal gray suit with a gray-and-black tie and she was wearing a long black dress with a matching black hat, and though he was standing of his own volition, I could tell that she was walking for him. His head was on her shoulder and her arm was about his waist, and as I watched the two of them slowly make their way down the long, narrow aisle, I could not help but think that I was no longer seeing the strong person of my childhood. Instead, I was gazing at the sad remnants of a broken soul.

I followed them with my eyes until they reached the front pew, where they sat just a few feet from the two bronze coffins. And as they sat, I heard the lady next to me sigh deeply and then I heard her say, "That poor man," and I saw her slowly shake her head, and when she did, a single tear rolled down her face, and I heard the woman sitting to her right say, "Thank God for Daphne," and I stole a quick glance at the two of them, and instantly, I realized that I did not know her or the lady with whom she was speaking.

I looked at them a moment, and then at Daphne, and I was thinking about Daphne, and how she had taken Luther in after his mother died, and how she had educated him, and how she had sent him off to the army to see the world and to learn a trade. And I was thinking how she had always been a constant in Luther's life, and how fortunate he was to have someone who loved him as she always had. And I was thinking about all of that when I heard the woman next to me speak again.

"You think he did it?" she asked, and there was a pained look on her face and hesitancy in her voice. And the woman with whom she was speaking did not respond and I sensed she was pondering the question.

And then I saw her lips part and her mouth open, and she finally ventured an answer. "I don't know," she said. "I just don't know."

Then I saw the other lady shake her head again and as she did, she looked toward the pew in which Luther and his aunt were sitting. I looked, too. Luther was leaning forward with his face buried in his hands, crying, and his Aunt Daphne was slowly rubbing her hand back and forth across his back. I looked only for a moment and then I turned away out of fear that I, too, would begin to cry. And as I diverted my eyes, there was in me a strong desire to go to him as it had once been my place to do, and I thought how strange it was in this, his hour of need, not to be able to do that which was still in me to do. I felt my spirits sway as I heard the distant moan of a somber soul cry out against the loss that had brought her here, and the wretched sound of her voice touched something within, and I realized at that moment, though I, too, had come to mourn the dead, it was the circumstances of their deaths that had brought me to this place which I had long ago put behind me. I recognized that I had not come because I had wanted to but because I had to see that he was all right.

And yet, as I witnessed his anguish and lamented the fact that I could not go to him, there was in me a terrible sadness that I could not shake. I sensed that he was dangling over the edge, perilously suspended somewhere between life and death, and that this burden which was now his to bear was one which he could not bear alone. And I knew that etiquette demanded that I give him time, and that there was a line that I should not cross, but the seriousness of the moment threatened to trump all that should be. I wanted only to feel the peace and security of knowing that he was safe. And I was thinking of my desires for him when I heard the drone of the organ and suddenly I was aware of the two ladies again, and I heard one say to the other, "The folks really turned out, didn't they?"

And again, I surveyed the room, and though I had expected a crowd, never could I have imagined the scene that was before me. The pews on either side of the sanctuary were filled, as were the seats in the balcony, and standing shoulder to shoulder along each wall were hordes of well-dressed people. In their midst were black folks and white folks, and old folks and young folks, and relatives and acquaintances, and through the rear door of the church, I could see yet others extending well beyond the entrance and out onto the church grounds. And this scene confused me, until I remembered that she was a teacher and that among those present were her students, and her colleagues, and her friends, and that the news of her murder had caused this entire town to mourn. And I remembered that a child had been killed, and that his death had been particularly difficult to understand, and I remembered that this was a small town, populated by folks who had an intimate knowledge of each other, and for them to think that one of their own could kill in such a vicious manner was beyond them, and I remembered that this was a church, and within its walls was the only place that many of them could go to understand something that seemed incomprehensible. And suddenly, I was aware of the music again. And the spirit of sadness was upon this place. I looked at Luther sitting well beyond the sea of mourners, and I again desired to go to him.

CHAPTER 10

The choir stopped singing and at that moment a billowing cloud of blackness swept toward my eyes and I was instantly transported to a time when Juanita and I were whole, and our child was happy, and our biggest concern was coping with the mundane trivialities of our day-to-day life. And oh, what I would not give at this very moment to have the problems of a week ago and to be free from this nightmare that was now my reality.

I heard the music again, and instinctively, I stared longingly at one coffin and then at the other. In the distance I heard the pained shout of some hurting soul and I heard feet scurrying toward the sound of her voice—and I knew it was the ushers hurrying to fan her quiet or to carry her outside. And I closed my eyes again, wishing that I could somehow still the ache that was now my heart. And I felt my hands trembling, and I felt my stomach flutter. And suddenly it was as if a hot ball of guilt rumbled from the pit of my stomach and lodged itself in the hollow of my throat, and my breath became short and my shoulders began to shudder, and I again wished that I could die. And I was engulfed in that feeling when the music stopped and I saw Reverend Thomas rise from his seat in the pulpit and walk to the edge of the platform. And I saw him open his mouth to speak and I could see his lips moving, but my mind could not grasp his words. And I felt myself drifting as if on a cloud, higher and higher, until I was above it all.

And I could see Juanita. And I could see little Darnell. And their eyes were closed, and I yelled to them, but there was something between us, and I could not rouse them. And I wanted to go to them. And I saw them drifting farther and farther away. And I could feel my spiraling spirits sink even lower. And I could not rise and I could not move. And there was total silence about me now, for suddenly, I could not hear. And my eyes were open, but I could no longer see. And I had a desire to yell out again, but suddenly, I could not speak. And the dimming light had faded to darkness. And suddenly there was loneliness where there had once been joy. And I sensed that everyone was looking at me, but I could not see them nor could I return their stares, for at the moment I was locked into an existence from which I could not rise. And my body was numb, and my mind was weary, and I could not focus on that which was around me. And I could not hold my shoulders back or my head up. And I could not control the muscles of my face, and I knew that my jaw had dropped and my eyes had become glazed. And mine was now a living form slumping under the weight of a heavy affliction.

And then I was aware of the sound of Reverend Thomas's voice again. And I raised my head, and I saw him standing back from the podium, and he was holding a white handkerchief in his hand and his brow was furrowed, and he was standing tall and straight and looking out over the congregation, and in his eyes was a distant stare—I could tell that he was not seeing us; instead, he was seeing the vivid images his words were creating.

"Late one night," I heard the lyrical words booming from his voice engulf the church, and when they did, he paused a minute, as if to let us know that he was in no hurry. For time was a tool whose value had ceased to have importance for those who now lay interred before his pulpit, and that one day, it would cease to have value for us, too.

He closed his eyes and shook his head and I saw a wry smile form at the corners of his mouth . . . "A few days ago" . . . he began to speak again . . . "God took death aside" . . . he paused again and opened his eyes . . . "And God told death to go to a little place

called Brownsville" . . . "Yes, I heard someone shout . . . " and find
a street called Turner Drive . . . "Well," came the shout of another
. . . "and on that street there's a little white house . . . " "My Lord,"
someone else exclaimed . . . "and in that house, you'll find the
Jackson family" . . . "Hallelujah," came another excited voice . . .
"and when you find them . . . tell Juanita Jackson I said: it's time
to come home."

The sound of my dead wife's name caused me to shudder, and
I closed my eyes against the image that Reverend Thomas was creating. Suddenly, I was standing before the door again, and the
smell of burning flesh was in my nostrils and the stench of death
was in my consciousness and my heart was racing and my eyes
were watering and the crux of my world was slipping beyond my
reach. And I did not want to relive this moment, and I told myself
to sit still and wait on Him that had promised me peace. After all,
this was His house, and He was more than capable. I leaned back
and I let my eyes drift past Reverend Thomas and they fell on the
large painting sitting high on the wall behind the choir, and in the
painting was Jesus and sitting with Him were his disciples, and
they were positioned behind a long table and on that table was a
basket of fruit, and they were eating and smiling, even as they sat
in the presence of death. And at that moment, I wanted what they
had. I wanted Him that held power over all things to speak to
peace. And I wanted Him to tell peace to come to me and to de-
liver me from the monstrous grip of misery that now held me firm
in its clutches. And I was praying to Him who sat at the center of
the table when I again became aware of someone else's voice.
"Praise God," they shouted. And then I heard Reverend Thomas's
voice.

". . . And then God paused a minute and he scratched his head.
And death turned to leave. And when he did, God beckoned him
back. And God said: Death . . . while you are there . . . tell little
Darnell I said come on, too . . ."

And Reverend Thomas paused, and when he did, I heard the
people yell, "Amen!" and I dropped my head and sobbed. And my
heart was aching and my head was throbbing, and all I wanted was

to die. And I heard my aunt whisper, "Help him, Jesus", and I felt
her hand rubbing my back again. And Darkness was all about me.
And I was again overcome by an intense feeling of loneliness. And
I heard Reverend Thomas's voice again, as if from a distant place;
and it was strong, and filled with the assurance of one certain of
the veracity of that about which he spoke. And though I was no
longer looking at him, I knew that he was standing at the edge of
the pulpit and he was looking at the coffins, and he was hearing
God, and God was talking to the rest of us through him.

"Tell them that I got this place" . . . Reverend Thomas paused
again. And I heard my aunt say, "Thank you, Jesus." And I heard
someone else shout, "Hallelujah" . . . and then I heard Reverend
Thomas resume . . . "Tell them that it's a place prepared just for
them . . . It's a place where time stands still . . . and where life triumphs over death . . . and good triumphs over evil . . . and death
went out at the speed of light . . . and when she got there, she
knocked on the door. And Juanita answered" . . . "Have mercy,"
someone shouted . . . "And death stretched forth her mighty
hand . . . and a bright light shone . . . and the rays of that light
rose from deep within the cradle of the earth and stretched forth
to the distant shores of heaven. And at the end of that light was
He who created the heavens and the earth. And he was draped in
raiment that shone of pure gold. And his hands, too, were
stretched forth. And his arms were open, and on his face was a
heavenly smile. And he beckoned to those for which He had sent.
Juanita tilted her head back and she looked up toward the hill
from which cometh her help. And her eyes beheld the glory of
the Lord. And tears of joy began to stream down her face . . . She
grabbed the hand of her child . . . and they both stretched their
hands forth toward the hand of the man who calmed the sea . . .
and God leaned back . . . and with one gentle tug, he lifted them
up toward heaven" . . . Reverend Thomas paused, then cupped
his hands over his eyes and looked up toward heaven . . . "Can't
you see them rising slowly?" . . . Then he lowered his head and
put one hand behind his ear . . . "Listen, saints" . . . He paused
again, then shook his head . . . "Can't you hear them shouting for

joy? . . . Can't you hear them praising God? . . . Oh, Hallelujah . . . Praise God . . . they done finally got over . . . they done took their seat in the New Jerusalem . . . they won't cry no more . . . they won't want no more . . . they at home now . . . and they got their foot under my master's table and their head on my master's lap . . . they got joy . . . and they got peace . . . Oh, one of these mornings . . . and it won't be long . . . you gone look for Thomas . . . and I, too, will be gone . . . I'm going to a place . . . prepared just for me . . . Oh, I'm so glad I got religion . . . it's gone be all right . . . Family . . . don't you worry . . . It's gone be all right . . . You'll see them again . . . on the other side of glory . . . Hallelujah . . . Praise God . . . It's gone be all right."

Reverend Thomas took his seat and I watched the undertaker remove the flowers and open the lids of both coffins, and from where I sat, I could see the profile of my wife and child's face, and I lowered my head again and sobbed, and all about me I could hear the throngs of people as they filed past the coffins. And though I wanted to raise my head and acknowledge them, I could not bring myself to look at that which I had not the strength to see. And as I heard them passing by, I silently began to pray for the strength to make it through this moment, and the courage to bid my family good-bye, and the ability to rise and walk out of this place on legs that I was not certain could hold me. And I was in the midst of that prayer when someone stopped before me, and I looked up, and Felicia was standing over me, and she touched my hand—and her touch was soft—no, gentle—and she said, "I'm sorry for your loss. And I will keep you in my prayers." And I shut my eyes against the warm tears streaming down my face. And I nodded my head and thanked her, and I watched her walk away. And then I saw the funeral director step forward to close the coffins, and the finality of it all dawned on me and suddenly I had trouble drawing another breath and I felt my body shaking again, and I felt my aunt's hand on my back, gently rubbing and caressing me, and I wanted to raise my hand and stop the moment. As futile as I knew it to be, I wanted to hold onto them as long as I could, and in my mind I saw myself leaping to my feet and hurling my body against the coldest of the coffins, and I heard myself pleading not to let this be, and suddenly an image appeared and I saw the two of them wave to me, and I heard Juanita's soft, gentle voice say, *Good-bye, Luther*, and I heard my son say, *'Bye Daddy*, and I saw them move away from me and I saw their bodies ascending toward the heavens, and I stretched forth my hands toward the both of them, and somewhere deep inside of me I heard myself scream, "I can't make it without you." And as I screamed, I felt my aunt's hand on me again, and heard her say, "Help him, Master." And the sound of her voice brought me back to the moment, and I was kneeling on the floor, and my hands were stretched toward the coffins and a crowd of folks had gathered around me. And suddenly, I had a sharp sense of the momentous pain consuming the entirety of my being. And I wanted but to die, and to ascend with them, for I knew at that very moment that there was nothing here that I either wanted or desired. And there was nothing here that could ever again sustain or comfort me. And I heard the weary voices around me saying that it was going be all right. And I closed my ears against their words and secretly wished that the beating of my heart would suddenly cease, for intuitively I knew, as did they, that things would never be right in my world again.

CHAPTER II

I touched Luther's hand and mumbled a few words to him and he looked up at me and I am not sure he recognized me. And I returned to my seat and watched the others file by the coffins and I was listening to one woman tell another what a good job the mortician had done with the bodies when above the music I heard the sound of a man's voice crying out for mercy and I looked toward the front of the church and Luther was kneeling on the floor with his hands stretched toward the coffins and his family was around him, and I could feel the depth of his pain, and my heart and my soul went out to him.

I cupped my hands over my eyes and I cried from a place that was once his, and I cried for all that he had lost and all that I knew he would go through, and I cried for the senselessness of this tragedy, and I cried for the sense of loss that was now the hardship so many would have to bear, and I thought of my mother, and I thought of my own life, and I thought of how short was this journey upon which we all had embarked and I vowed that from this moment on I would live life to its fullest and I would love with an intensity rooted in the understanding that to love was to live. And I would pray for him and his family—and I would pray unceasingly until this burden that was now theirs to shoulder had passed.

I kept my head bowed down in prayer until I heard the coffins roll past. Then I rose and followed the others out of the church and joined the long procession of cars as it slowly wound its way from the church grounds through the narrow streets to the highway, and finally toward the quaint cemetery neatly nestled at the far end of the community in which most of us lived. And as we drew near to our destination, I broke from the procession and drove the short distance to my mother's house, and I parked my car on the street beyond her yard and walked back to the cemetery. And when I arrived, I saw Reverend Thomas move to the edge of the grave and open his Bible, and I heard him begin to read the twenty-third psalm, and for the first time, I looked at Juanita's mother. She was sitting next to her husband, and her hands were folded across her lap and her eyes were staring blankly ahead and suddenly I felt sorry for her. I did not know her. She was not from Brownsville and neither was her husband. But I knew that Juanita was her only child, and that the two of them had been extremely close, and that she was having a difficult time coping with the prospect of life without her. And I was thinking of the two of them when I heard the sound of a lone bird singing in the distance, and as I looked toward the sound, I saw a tiny sparrow perched high upon the limb of a live-oak tree, and suddenly, I could not help but think how beautiful was the sound and how peaceful was this place. And I looked past the stand of oak trees and my eyes fell upon the spattering of wildflowers and the plush green pasture in the distance with its rolling hills and grazing cattle; and I could not help but notice the feel of the afternoon sun as it warmed the side of my face, and the warmth of her rays and the beauty of her light spoke to me as if from another existence, reminding me of the vibrancy of this thing called life.

And I was taking it all in when I again became aware of the sound of Reverend Thomas's voice: "And let us be reminded," he said, "that it is not the end but only a brief separation until we can all be together again in a place of even greater peace and greater beauty, for though the day seems dark, in time the sun will shine again."

And then I saw him reach down and retrieve a handful of dirt, and I heard him say, "Ashes to ashes . . . and dust to dust." Then I saw him gingerly sprinkle dirt on Juanita's coffin and then on that of her son. Then I heard Reverend Thomas ask the Lord to take these two souls unto his kingdom and then I heard him ask the Lord to be with the family in this, their time of need. Then he asked us all to remember this day and to love each other as God loves us, and to be mindful of the fact that tomorrow is not promised. Then I saw those standing around the grave turn to leave, and my eyes again fell upon Luther and I started to move toward him again, but as I did, I saw one of the uniformed officers make his way toward the chairs in which he, his aunt, and Juanita's parents were sitting. And when he was near, I saw the officer embrace Juanita's mother and whisper something in her ear, and she nodded, and I looked at Luther sitting next to her. His eyes were locked on the coffins sitting beside the two freshly dug graves, and I noticed that the officer did not look at Luther nor did Luther look at the officer. And I decided that under the circumstances, it was probably best that I leave.

CHAPTER 12

I saw the uniformed officer approaching us but I refused to look
at him. Instead, I kept my eyes focused on the two deep holes
into which my loved ones were about to be lowered, and again I
wished that time would halt, and that the heavens would open,
and that He would speak, and that this terrible nightmare would
be no more.

And I knew that for which I wished could come to pass, for I
knew that He who made time could also make time stand still.
And I knew that He who took life could also give it. I was waiting
for a miracle when I saw the officer bend and embrace Juanita's
mother, and I heard him say, "I'm sorry for your loss." And I tried
not to listen to his words. I knew he meant well, but it was too
soon to accept what he was offering. I continued to stare at the
coffins and pray that He who could, would speak to the wind, and
that the wind would speak to the bones, and that the bones
would rattle and the lid would open and my family and I would be
one again.

And out of the corner of my eye, I saw her nod her head, ac-
knowledging his words, and I concentrated on the mounds of
earth and inside of me I could hear myself beseeching Him to
speak to the bones and as I pleaded with Him, I was suddenly
aware that those who came to honor the dead had turned away,
and I feared that they had given up and I wanted to yell at them to

wait, for any second now I knew that He who could, would speak to the wind, and the wind would speak to the bones.

Inside, I felt myself pressing Him harder, to move now before it was too late, and I closed my eyes against the movement of those who would leave, and I yielded to Him that could, and while I was waiting on that which I knew would happen, I heard the officer speaking again to her who had lost as much as I, and in his low, trembling voice was the pain of one who felt deeply, perhaps even more deeply than I would have cared to imagine.

"We will catch the monster that did this," he said. "As God is my witness, I promise you we will."

I was still waiting on Him that could to speak to the wind when I felt my aunt's hand on my arm, pulling me to my feet. And I pulled away from her, and fell once again to my knees, and I waited for Him that could to speak to the wind. And I heard my aunt say, "Help him, Master," and I felt the firm hand of one of the deacons on my arm and I felt him pulling me to my feet, and I felt myself struggling against those who would lead me from this place before He that could had done that which I knew He would. Suddenly, I felt myself tire, and I heard the deacon say, as if from some distant plane: "Lean on Him, son . . . just lean on Him . . . He can fix it . . . Just lean on Him." Then I felt myself surrender, for I knew at that moment, that He who could, had done all that He would. And there was an anger rising in me against all that I had ever heard, and all that I had ever believed about Him that could, for in this, my moment of need, He had forsaken me, and I felt myself railing against Him, and His world and His people and their beliefs and I wanted to strike out at something or someone so that they, too, could hurt as I hurt. And in the midst of this inner turmoil, I looked back at the coffins sitting next to the open graves, and I cried from a place deep within me, and I felt the strength from my legs give way, and I leaned on my aunt and I leaned on the deacon and their legs became my legs, and I felt myself moving farther away from all that remained of those whom I loved and I began to tremble and I bowed my head and once again I spoke to Him that could and asked him to please speak to the wind and ask the wind to speak to the bones.

And when I lifted my head, I was standing before the limo, and the deacon who had walked for me pulled the door open and I climbed inside and moved against the far door, and I gave in to the pain that now had hold of me, and suddenly, I felt my aunt's hand on my knee, and I heard Juanita's parents climb inside the vehicle and though I did not look at them, I could hear her mother crying and I could hear her father trying to comfort her and in the stillness of the moment, I was consumed by the feeling that things would never be normal again, and that sobering thought caused the warm tears to run. And I closed my eyes, and in the darkness of the moment I felt the car ease forward and I felt the hard, dry earth give way beneath the tires as the limo driver slowly navigated the car through the cemetery and out into the streets.

CHAPTER 13

My eyes were full of tears and they blurred, then I gasped, feeling the fullness of the sad scene unfolding before me. And in the midst of my crying, I spied the officer looking at Luther again. And I had a bewildering impulse to go to him and ask him to leave. But before I could, I saw him turn and walk away, and though he said nothing, I was troubled by the ominous look I saw in his eyes, and I was thinking of that officer as I watched the long black limousine pull out into the street. And I was wondering whether he had come to pay his respects to the dead or had he come out of some sinister need to assure Luther that he was watching him, and that this was not the end. It was only the beginning.

I made my way out of the cemetery and into the streets. It had been a long time since I had walked along the neighborhood, and I had forgotten what a strange neighborhood it was. The homes were an odd mix. A brick house here, a trailer there, and a spattering of wood-frame houses dispersed conspicuously on tiny lots that ran parallel to each other on narrow streets that sported no sidewalks, only drainage ditches and narrow shoulders. Like the hordes of others leaving the cemetery, I made my way out into the street and began the short trek back to Turner Drive, and as I moved beyond the borders of the cemetery, there flashed a quick image of the ambulance again, and through the slightly tinted window I could see Luther sitting next to his aunt, and suddenly I realized that this entire ordeal had pulled from me emotions I thought I had long buried, and the fact that those emotions were bubbling toward the surface caused me to contemplate matters that I had long tried to forget. And in my moment of contemplation, I was glad that I had decided to walk. The feel of the road beneath my feet had a calming effect, and somehow the passing moments seemed slower, and my thoughts seemed clearer, and the fullness of the day seemed slightly lighter and less congested. And my mind was no longer fixated on the horrible events of the moment; instead, I found myself struggling to understand the events of my life that had brought me to this day.

Like Luther, I had been married for nearly twenty years. But for the vast majority of those years, my husband and I had not been as two people bound in marriage should have been, and only now as I walked along the narrow road toward the home of my childhood, did I realize that I had not been able to be as I should have been with my husband because my heart never truly belonged to him. I also realized that I had gotten married simply to drown myself in the affection of a man who did adore me, even as I tried to forget him that I adored.

And now that I am in this place again, I find that my heart is once again reeling for him who I must now watch endure the pain of losing the love which he long ago chose over me. Suddenly, in the dimness of it all, I was besieged by an image born back in times that only I could see. We were alone, and he had just told me that he had fallen in love with her. And I was remembering the sound of my trembling voice, and the pain of my broken heart, and the frantic tenor of my feeble pleas as I begged him not to end that which I felt was destined to be. And I was remembering the sordid details of my emotional breakdown on that somber July day—some twenty-three years ago, when my mother put me on a train for California because she realized that I could no longer exist in a world in which I could see him and not be with him, and I was remembering begging not to be sent away, and crying for days on end, and dreaming of him as often as I slept. And now in this, his hour of torment, I, too, am still tormented, for as he hurt, I hurt; and I wished that this nightmare would soon pass, and that he could rise again and stand on legs firmly committed to moving on with a life which he no longer wanted to live.

Just before me, I could see a man and his wife; and like me, the two of them were walking the short distance back to the quarters. They were holding hands and she was crying, and upon his face I saw a look of somber resignation, and I knew that they had been moved by the funeral, and now that it was over, they, too, were trying to make sense of what appeared to be senseless. Suddenly, I looked beyond them and I followed the path of the ambulance with my eyes. From the route the driver had taken, I suspected that Luther was on his way home, and in the midst of that realization the tiny voice inside of my head spoke to me again.

Go to him, it said. *He needs you.*

Then, in the gathering dusk, I felt myself reeling at the possibility of being next to him again. But was it that simple? Could I go to him in spite of all that had happened? Again the image of him came to me, and his weary body was leaning gently against my body, and my arm was about his shoulder, and his head was resting upon my breast, and I was holding him with tenderness, and the vision of this moment caused my flesh to tingle. And then, as suddenly as that image appeared, it dissipated, and I heard the voice of reason say, *No, the time is not right*. And I wanted to blot out that voice and hold on to that image. And suddenly, I was again aware of the war waging inside of me, and I could not bear to think of how it would be not to go to him. So I pushed the thought of him away from me just as I had done for all of these years, and I was aware of the silence surrounding me. Then my mind cleared, and I was again aware of mother's house standing before me.

I went inside, changed clothes, and stood before the window. Behind me, I could hear the soft, steady sound of my mother sleeping.

CHAPTER 14

I heard my aunt tell the limo driver to drop me off first. I had made it clear to her that I wanted to go home and be alone in the place where my family had last been whole. When the driver was close, he pulled the limo to the shoulder, and I turned my face toward the house and cast my eyes upon the door. In the streets beyond the limo, I heard the innocent laughter of a child playing nearby; and the sound of the child's voice seeped into my consciousness, and at that moment, I could not imagine ever laughing again. Then, in the midst of that thought, I heard Mrs. Miller whimpering again. I turned and looked at her. She had placed her head gently upon her husband's shoulder and though her eyes were fixed in my direction, she was not looking at me; instead, she was looking beyond me. And in that instant, I realized I had not considered her feelings in my request to be taken to the very spot where she had last seen her child, and that realization caused my lips to part, and I heard myself say, "I'm sorry," and when I did, Mr. Miller slowly raised his eyes, and when our eyes met, he did not speak. And I sensed that now, more than ever before, he was blaming me. Suddenly, I dropped my eyes and grabbed the door handle in preparation to exit the limousine, but before I pushed the door open, the sound of my aunt's voice stopped me.

"I wish you would come back to my house," she said. "I don't feel comfortable leaving you alone like this."

"I just want to go home," I said.

"You need to be with family," she said.

"I'll be all right," I said. I closed the door and when I did, my aunt lowered the window.

"Are you sure?" she said, and in her eyes was the same concern I had seen my entire life.

"I'm sure," I said.

She looked at me for a moment.

"If you need me," she said, "you know where I'll be."

I nodded and watched the limousine pull out into the street and slowly disappear into the distant curve. No sooner was it gone, than I crossed the yard and climbed the steps leading onto the porch. When I opened the door and stepped inside, I instinctively paused. In my mind I was waiting for some evidence that they were still there. But now, where there had once been the sounds of life, silence existed. And I wanted desperately to see the dull glare of the television, or smell the fresh scent of chicken frying. And I wanted to hear her ask me about my day, and I wanted to hear my son tell me all about his. When I heard nothing, I wanted to holler out for them, and just as I was about to scream, my eyes fell on the spot where they had lain, and though my aunt had cleaned the house immaculately, I could see the image of them just as clearly as I had seen them that night. Inside, I felt my heart raging against the demon that had taken them away, and I told myself that this was but a bad dream. So I slammed the door behind me and I made my way to my son's room. I pushed the door open and I called to him gently, and when he did not answer, I paused again, then I called to him a second time, softly, tenderly. "Son, where are you?"

I made my way to our room and looked at the bed upon which she and I had lain, and in the center was her gown, and on the floor near the foot of the bed were her slippers, and I called to her and in the silence of the moment, I began to cry again. And like a madman, I raced from room to room, looking for one and then the other. And in the midst of my search, I felt die in me again the hope which had died a thousand times before. Outside her door, I felt myself take one step and then another, and my legs were trying to tell me to stop. But I fought the impulse to give in to that which I knew I could not accept and I leaned against the wall and followed the long hallway out into the parlor, and my eyes fell on Juanita's favorite chair and in my mind, I could see her sitting with her back to me and her face was toward the fireplace; and there was a peaceful contentment about her, and I smiled for I knew now that I could go to her, and I stepped toward her image, and in an instant the image vanished, and my spirits sank. But I pressed on, moving from the parlor to the kitchen and from the kitchen to the laundry room, and in each room, I looked behind doors and checked inside closets and pulled back window curtains. I checked the bathrooms and the storeroom, and went outside and back inside, and I finally gave in and slumped on the bed in the room where my search had begun. I was numb, my head was swirling, and my stomach was aching; I wanted but to curl into a tight ball and close my eyes against the pain I knew I could not bear much longer. And there was this longing in me, and I prayed for sleep to come. And I prayed for the peace and solitude one finds when one's body and mind are at rest, and the soul drifts to another dimension—the dimension of the unconscious. That was where I longed to be. In a state where I see nothing; I hear nothing; I know nothing.

CHAPTER 15

The light was on across the street, and through the thinly veiled window I could see him standing half naked before the mirror. There was a moment, come suddenly upon me, in which I could recall when he was mine, and I was his, and that was not strange to me, for though I was forty years old and had lived without him for much of my adult life, I had not ceased to think of him. Not even as I departed this place for the bright lights of the city and he remained here in his beloved Brownsville, and not even as I exchanged vows with another man and he with another woman.

And yet though I longed to cross the narrow street that separated us, I knew that the time was still not right. And thus, I could only stand before the window, as I had, off and on, for the past few weeks since my return, in the living room of the place of my childhood, staring and longing, and praying. My heart was heavy and my soul was sad. I wished that there was something I could do other than watch from a distance as the only man whom I had ever truly loved endured that which he should not endure alone. I was confused and ashamed by what I felt, for there was a sort of eagerness in me—a sense of anticipation, and that should not be. His wife and child were recently killed; so was my husband, yet I could not think of them, I could only think of him, and the opportunity that existed for us to straighten out that which should have never gone awry. And, then, in a moment of clarity, I tried to shake those feelings, but the sight of him standing half dressed before the mirror dislodged something within me, and in that instant, I was no longer a forty-year-old widow, home to care for her ailing mother; instead, I was young and pure again, and my pristine body was craving the tender touch of him that would introduce me to the foreign world of womanhood. And the hour was late, and he and I were alone, and I was lying on his bed, clad only in my panties, and the lights were low, and the music was soft, and he was lying next to me and his strong but gentle hands were slowly caressing the contours of my half naked body and I could feel the warmth of his breath on the side of my neck, and suddenly, my eyes are closed against the yearning that his touch had aroused in me. I felt his mouth next to my ear, and I heard him whisper, ever so softly, *Are you sure?*

I was sure that this was the moment, and he was the one, and the fact that he was made this all right within me. Yes I would give to him that which I had saved for the one who would be mine— not simply in my moment of giving but for all eternity. I heard myself whisper, *Yes, I am sure*.

I surrendered myself to him, and in the moment of my surrender, I hear the bedsprings creak and I felt the weight of his body on top of mine. I ran my hand across the small of his back and there was upon me a strange surge of emotion as I felt the gentle caress of his full, moist lips upon the nape of my neck, and I knew that this, my entry into womanhood, was not as my parents would have wished things to be. They would have preferred that he and I were married, and that we were together not in the heat of a cheapened moment, but that we were on a romantic island in our bridal suite overlooking the pure white sands of some distant beach, and that as a prelude, he and I had spent the day together in matrimonial anticipation, walking hand and hand with the wind in our hair and the ocean at our feet. And that this moment for me was as special as it could be for one who had seen the value of giving to him with whom she was besotted, a love that was as pure as any love that one person could give to another. Yet, I was happy with my choice to give my body to this man, on this day, at this time, and I only wished that my hands were more experienced, and that I could, through a simple touch, reveal to him the depth of what I felt for him.

Somehow, even in my clumsiness, the moment of our love was slow and gentle, filled with the passion of two people destined to be, and the sounds of his panting, and the motion of his loins, unleashed in me all that I had hoped the moment would bring, and as the roll of his hips shuddered still, I felt break in me emotions which until that moment I knew not that I possessed. And I knew from that moment on, I was his to do with as he pleased, and I also knew what I had just given to him, I would give to no other. And I was thinking of that moment as I watched him standing half naked before the mirror across the street.

And suddenly, I could not help but notice the stillness of the night, or the way the huge branches of the old oak tree in the yard before his house hung perfectly still in the evening heat of the breezeless air. Or the spot where, in our youth, he and I had stood beneath that same tree on a starlit night, and kissed for the very first time. And I was looking at that spot, remembering the youthful exuberance I felt at the moment our lips first touched, when I heard the feeble sound of my mother's voice behind me. I turned and looked—her eyes were open, and her frail, sick body lay motionless on the old, tattered sofa. Yes, she was awake now, and she seemed perturbed that I was still standing where I had stood when she dozed off more than an hour ago.

"You still standing in that window?" she asked with a dash of perturbed brevity.

"Yes, ma'am," I said.

"I guess he's still over there?" she said, and in her eyes I could see that she was not concerned with Luther, or with what was transpiring across the street; she was concerned with what was transpiring within me.

"He's still there," I said.

And when I did, I saw her frown and rub her temple.

"Well, I don't know why he would want to stay in that house

after everything that's happened," she said. "It just don't seem natural."

And though I heard her, I did not say anything. I turned back toward the window and gazed out into the streets. It had still been light out when I returned from the cemetery, but now the sun had set, and a few stars were out, and the entire street lay silent under the long, flickering shadows cast by the street lamps and I sensed that everyone on the block was anxiously sitting behind locked doors, worrying that the killer who had invaded Luther's house might also invade theirs. Everyone—that is, except Luther. His family was gone and he was in a perpetual daze, sitting in semidarkness, apparently longing for faces he could no longer see.

"The police were over there again today," she said, after a moment or two. "I guess they still trying to figure out what happened?"

"Well, when they do," I said, "maybe it will give him some peace." I turned back toward the window. Luther had moved from before the mirror and was now sitting on the edge of the bed. His head was bowed and it appeared that once again, he was crying. "I feel so sorry for him," I said. "This is more than anyone should have to bear."

"Maybe you feeling sorry for the wrong one," my mother said. "Two people are dead. Maybe they're the ones you should feel sorry for."

"Feeling sorry for them won't help much," I said. "They're gone. He still has to live."

"He'll live," she said, looking at me with her big gray eyes. "You can count on that."

"I hope you're right," I said.

"I'm right," she said. "I just pray he didn't have anything to do with this."

"He didn't," I said.

"Well, the police seem to think he did."

"They're wrong," I said.

"And what if they're not?"

"They are," I said, with a tinge of anger in my slightly elevated voice.

There was silence. She frowned. I saw her eyes cloud.

"You're still stuck on him, aren't you?"

I didn't answer.

"I don't want you over there," she said. "You hear?"

I remained silent.

"I mean it," she said. "I don't want you over there."

"I just need to know he's okay."

"Why? He's not your concern."

"I almost married him," I said. "Or have you forgotten?"

"Thank God you didn't," Mother said, shaking her head as she spoke, and I could tell she was remembering all that had transpired between Luther and me.

"Sometimes I wish I had." I said.

"I don't know why you would wish such a thing."

"Because it's true."

"You married well," she said.

"No," I said. "I married rich. There's a difference."

"Clarence was a good man. And he provided you with a good life. Why would you wish that away? Why?"

"Clarence didn't love me. He just loved what I looked like."

"I don't believe that."

"You ought to believe it," I said, "because it's the truth."

"Well, love or not, he was good to you."

"And I was good to him," I said. "But I wasn't in love with him. I was in love with Luther. And I think you know that."

"Have you forgotten what he did to you?"

I turned back toward the streets and looked out into the vast nothingness. I didn't want to talk about this any longer.

"Have you?" she asked again.

"No, ma'am," I said. "I haven't forgotten."

"You act like you have."

"Well, I haven't," I said.

I paused and I saw my mother slowly shaking her head.

"I'm sorry I had to ask you to come back here," she said.

"Maybe it's fate," I said.

"Is that what you think?"

"God works in mysterious ways," I said. "Isn't that what you've always taught me?"

"I'm old," she said. "And I'm sick. And I don't have the strength to go through this again. I just don't."

Suddenly, she paused and her eyes widened.

"What's the matter?" I asked.

"Somebody's at the door," she whispered.

"All right," I said. "I'll get it."

CHAPTER 16

"Watch out for the begonias."

Those were the first words she ever uttered to me. It was the summer of '79. I was mowing their lawn and my mind was not on my work as it should have been, and she came storming out of the house.

"You must be careful," Juanita said, and her soft, delicate voice reflected no anger, but it was filled with concern. "The begonias are my mother's prize possession."

I heard her but I was not as conscious of her as I was the large, beautiful begonia bush that I had come so close to ruining.

"Yes, ma'am," I said. "I will." And she laughed at me.

"Do I look like a *ma'am* to you?" she asked.

I had not really looked at her when she first spoke to me. But now, I turned my head and looked at her closely. I was stunned. She was seventeen, maybe eighteen, I supposed. She had shoulder-length hair, big, beautiful brown eyes, and a tiny mole above her lip on the left side of her face. Her hair was down, and I could not help thinking that she was one of the most beautiful women I had ever seen. She saw me looking at her and I quickly looked away.

"Well?" she said.

"No, ma'am," I said nervously.

She laughed again and I grimaced, feeling certain that I was making a fool of myself. I was surprised by this reaction in me. I

had a girl and we were happy. And I was thinking that I shouldn't
be looking at her. So, I kept my face averted and I assured her that
I would be careful, and with that assurance she turned and walked
away and I was certain that was the end of it. But a few weeks
later, I was breaking up with my girlfriend, and she and I were a
couple.

"I miss you so much." I heard her voice again, and I raised my
head from the bed and looked about the room, seeking to glimpse
the face from which the words came. I saw nothing. So I rose to
my feet in front of the large mirror before which she so often
dressed and I mumbled, "I miss you, too." Then I paused and
waited for her to speak to me again, but when no words came, I
called to her once more. "Juanita." I paused again and I looked
about, wide-eyed. Then, above the silence, I heard her voice again.
"Come to me," it said. "Please come to me." And I felt my body
reeling, and I felt the room shaking, and I could make no sense of
what I was hearing. I looked deep into the mirror, and in the dimness of my own reflection, I saw her vague image floating as if suspended in time, beckoning me toward her, and I squinted, confused
by what I was seeing. "Where are you?" I said, and the floating
image of her began to fade and I leaned toward the mirror and
called to her, and she replied, "Come to me." Then I watched her
image become smaller and smaller. "NO!" I screamed at the top of
my lungs and I grabbed the mirror with both hands, and I held on
tight with trembling fingers, and the image continued to fade
until finally, it was gone. And when it was gone, I felt myself sink-
ing, back into the depths of the deep, dark, bottomless pit in
which I had existed since this tragedy occurred.

What did this mean? What was she trying to tell me? Why had
she come, only to leave again? I stood before the mirror, hoping
that she would return once more. And as I waited, I thought of
something. Suddenly, it all made sense. "Come to me." Yes, now I
understood. And because I did, I felt my spirits being lifted. It was
not possible for her to join me in my world, but I could join her in
hers. And thus, she had spoken to me from beyond the grave.
And now I knew.

Yes, it was meant to be, and now, I had only to act. But, how? Suddenly, I felt my heart pounding. I opened one drawer and then another. I was not sure. And then, I saw it tucked neatly beneath her underwear in the far corner of the bottom dresser drawer. And I removed the gun and placed it on the dresser. My head was swirling, and the fire in the pit of my stomach was raging. And I stood back and stared at it. And there was no fear in me now, only the eager anticipation of seeing them again. Then, for some reason, I turned my head toward my bedroom window. Outside, dusk had fallen, and the streetlight was on, and there was an odd quietness about. And for a moment, I gazed at the only world I had ever known, fully expecting never to see it again. Then, I retrieved the gun, and placed the barrel squarely against the side of my head. And I stared into the mirror seeing again her fading image, and I smiled, for, as she had requested, I was about to come to her.

CHAPTER 17

I made my way to the wooden door leading onto the porch, and I pulled the curtain back and peeped through the window. A strange man was standing on the top step just beyond the screen door. He was wearing a suit and tie and carrying a pad, and I figured it had something to do with what had happened across the street. I thought about not answering, but then I realized that what he had to say might shed some light on things. The door swung open and he smiled; and I smiled back at him.

"May I help you?" I asked.

"Good evening, ma'am," he said, and I looked past him toward Luther's house. I could still see Luther. Only now, he was no longer sitting on the edge of the bed. He was standing before the dresser, staring into the large mirror. I looked back at the strange white man standing before me. He was much younger than I first thought.

"It sure is a hot one," he said.

I wiped my hands on the hem of my apron.

"It's been that way all week," I said. Then I saw him began fiddling with his bag.

"My name is Brown," he said. "Cleo Brown. And I'd like to speak to you about a special we're running on magazine subscriptions, if I may."

"You're a salesman."

"No, ma'am," he said. "I'm a college student. This is how I pay for my tuition. I sell magazines during the summer and work odd jobs during the year."

"Oh, I see," I said.

"Would you like to purchase a subscription?" he said.

"I'm not interested."

"It's only five dollars a month."

"Maybe some other time."

"You don't have to pay for it right now," he said. "And if you change your mind, you can cancel the subscription within ten business days. No obligation on your part at all, but I would still get credit for the sale."

"I don't think so," I said.

"Are you sure?"

"I'm sure," I said, again. "Maybe some other time."

He paused and removed a handkerchief from his shirt pocket, and then wiped the sweat from his brow. "It sure is hot," he said again. I saw him looking past me into the house. "May I trouble you for a glass of water?"

"It's no trouble," I said.

I went into the house, and when I returned with the water, the man had climbed onto the porch, removed his shoes, and was massaging his foot.

"I don't mean to be rude," he said, "but my feet are killing me. I feel like I've walked a country mile today."

I didn't answer him. I handed him the glass and he tilted his head back and gulped the water down. When he was done, he handed the glass back to me and busied himself with his shoes.

"Sure you won't reconsider?" he said. "I'm prepared to knock an additional ten percent off the price if you do."

"I'm sure," I said, then I heard him sigh.

"Well, if that's the case, I guess I better be moving on." He rose to his feet, then paused. "Thank you for the water," he said. "And for your time."

"You're welcome," I said.

He turned to leave. Across the street, a car pulled to the shoulder and stopped. I watched the door swing open on the driver's side, and I saw Luther's aunt amble out and make her way across the yard and onto the porch. She was carrying a plate of food, neatly wrapped in foil, and I knew Luther would not eat. I knew he would place the plate on the dining table next to the window, and after she had left, he would sit before the plate and would stare absently out into the night, and perhaps he would swallow a bite or two before rising to his feet and retiring to his bedroom, where he had spent most of his time since returning from the funeral.

And I was thinking of this when a shot rang out. Then, a yellow flare flashed and I saw Luther fall headlong to the floor. I froze, stunned, my eyes glazed. My knees buckled, and I felt myself running toward the street. When I reached the edge of his porch, I stopped. Inside the house, I could hear his aunt talking. I paused a moment, then climbed the stairs and went inside. He was lying on the floor, the gun was in his hand, and a pool of blood had collected near his head. His eyes were closed his legs were twitching.

"Oh my God!" I heard his aunt say. "Help me!"

I looked at him, then at her. "Call an ambulance," I said. She hurried to the phone and I knelt next to him; then, I gently lifted his head and placed my ear next to his mouth. "Hurry!" I shouted. "He's not breathing." I tilted his head back and pinched his nose. I placed my mouth against his mouth. Our lips touched and I gently blew air into his lungs. I paused, then looked. Nothing.

I quickly laid my hands on top of his chest, one over the other, and I pressed hard. Then I counted, then I blew air in his lungs again, and pressed again, then counted again and pressed again. And I heard his aunt on the phone, and suddenly time stood still, and I was aware of the darkness about me, and the tiny beads of sweat forming in the center of my brow; and I was aware of the sound of people gathering in the street, and I was aware of his closed eyes, and his lifeless body, and I heard his aunt say, "Hold on, Luther, help is on the way." And I felt myself asking God to help me. I pressed and blew, and I pressed and I blew, and I felt time slowly seeping toward an ugly future, and my hands began to shake and my lips began to quiver, and I began to fear that my efforts were in vain, and then, in the distance, I heard the faint sound of the sirens. And I pressed and blew. And I pressed and blew. And then I saw the tips of his fingers move ever so slightly. And I felt his chest rise, then fall. And my lips were against his lips. And I heard the faint sound of his feeble voice say, "Juanita . . ."

CHAPTER 18

My lips parted and I heard myself whisper her name, and I struggled to open my eyes, to lift my hand, but I could not move. I was weak; and I felt faint, and I sensed that I was firmly in the grips of a force much stronger than I. And I fought against the force, and in the midst of my struggling, I heard the sirens again and felt the vibrations of heavy feet pounding the surface on which I lay, and I heard my aunt's voice riding gently on the stale, hot air. And then there were hands on me, and I felt my skin being pricked and my body being lifted; and then I heard my aunt's voice again. "Is he going to make it?" she asked. And though I did not know, I sensed that she was speaking of me. But where was I? What was this all about? I willed my eyes to open, but they would not. And because they would not, I felt myself become agitated, and I struggled against a brain that was now refusing my commands. Inside, I felt my heart racing. My breath was short. I tried to speak, but no sound would come. Then, suddenly, I was remembering again. And in that moment, I was seeing myself standing before the mirror. I was feeling my trembling fingers squeezing the trigger. I was hearing the gunfire and seeing myself slowly falling toward my bedroom floor. But where was I now?

Suddenly, I heard the man say "Ready . . . lift . . . " and I felt the bed rise and snap shut and I felt myself being rolled on squeaky wheels. "Careful," I heard the other one say. "Easy," came the voice of the other. Then there was a bump, and the sound of doors being shut, and the sound of the siren, and the feel of the road beneath the rubber tires. Where were they taking me? I felt myself reeling again. I desired to speak but I could not.

"Relax," I heard the voice of a white man.

Then I saw her again. She was looking and waiting, and upon her face was a look of extreme disappointment. "Juanita," I called to her softly. But she did not answer and I saw a tear in her eye, and I knew that once again I had failed her. *Come to me,* I heard her say again. And I struggled to move, and when I could not, I saw her image begin to fade. And as she faded to nothingness I heard myself say, "I'm sorry . . . I am so sorry."

Then, I was aware of them again and I could hear the loud, shrill sound of the blaring siren, and I could feel the ambulance weaving in and out of traffic, and I could feel my aunt's hand clutching my hand, and I could hear her soft, sweet voice praying to God and asking him to see me through this terrible time. Then my mind drifted back to dying, and I wished they would allow me to do that which I had set out to do.

And as the darkness engulfed me, I felt myself becoming weak and I felt something within drifting beyond me. Then things began to slow; my breathing began to ease, and I sensed that which I longed for was within my grasp. I heard my aunt scream, and then I heard the paramedic tell the driver to hurry, and I felt the ambulance accelerate, and I felt the heavy bump as the wheels sped over the railroad tracks, and I knew the hospital was very close, and I could hear my aunt asking God to hold me just a little while longer, and I closed my ears against her prayers and asked the Lord to let me come home to live with my family—today, tomorrow, and forever.

CHAPTER 19

They were gone and I was alone in his house. I looked about. The house was so different from what I remembered when he and I were dating. Back then it had belonged to his parents—it had been a small, wood-frame house sparsely decorated and in desperate need of repair. But now, it had been remodeled and there was a simple elegance about the place. There were pictures of them and their son, and there were beautiful hardwood floors, and expensive paintings, and elegant flowers and plants, perfectly placed, and I could see that his wife had been a caring person who paid a great deal of attention to detail. I was admiring their house and imagining their life in it when I heard someone calling my name. I turned and looked. It was T-Baby.

"You found him?" he asked me.

"No," I said. "His aunt."

I saw him remove his hat and wipe his brow.

"He say anything?"

"Just called her name."

"Whose name?" he said, and I saw him furrow his brow.

"His wife's name," I said. "Juanita."

And after I did, I looked around the room. I felt strange. She was dead. Savagely murdered. Yet, I was jealous of her, and the kind of life it appeared she had with Luther.

"Did he say anything else?"

"No," I said. "At least, not to me."

Suddenly, my eyes fell on an old recliner tucked away in the far corner. It was the only piece of furniture I recognized. It had belonged to Luther's father. I could remember seeing his father sitting in that chair, smoking his pipe while watching the evening news on television, and making fun of me and Luther, saying that we were too young to always be sitting around the house like an old married couple. It didn't surprise me that he had kept his father's chair. The two of them had been close before the hunting accident.

"Where was his aunt when you came in?" T-Baby asked me. He had removed a pad from his pocket and had moved to the far side of the room.

"Stooped over his body."

"Where was the gun?"

"In Luther's hand."

"Did his aunt say anything to you?"

"No," I said. "She was hysterical. I told her to call an ambulance."

He paused again and wrote something on the pad.

"Where were you when the gun went off?"

"Across the street," I said, "talking to a salesman."

"And his aunt?"

"She had just arrived," I said. "She was standing on his porch."

I saw him pause and write something on the tablet. As he did, my eyes began to stray. There was a fireplace in the living room now and beautiful drapes about the window. There was a sliding glass door that opened onto a small patio garden, none of which was there when he and I were dating.

"This place sure is different," I said, and when I did, I saw T-Baby raise his head and look in one direction, then the other.

"You can say that again," he said. "Between her money and his hard work, they really made a nice home out of this place. Shoot. I can remember when this was the worst little shack on the block. Now it just might be the best little house in the whole neighborhood." He paused again and shook his head. "That's why this all seems so strange to me. They worked so well together and they seemed to have had a good life. It's just hard to understand why he would do something like this."

"He," I said. "He, who?"

"Forget it," he said, and I saw him turn his attention back to the pad.

"No," I said. "Tell me."

He shook his head. "I've said too much as it is."

"We're old friends," I said. "We grew up together."

"Friends or not," he said.

"T-Baby," I said. "Please."

I heard him sigh deeply and then I saw him look up from the pad. Our eyes met and his face became stern.

"Look," he said, "this is bad and I think you know it." He paused again as if waiting for me to say something. I remained quiet and he began again. "And I think he knew it. I'm sure that's why he put that gun to his head," he said. "He didn't want to face what he knew was coming."

"Why are you talking in the past tense?" I said. "Don't you think he's going to make it?"

He looked away and shook his head. "Don't know," he said. "Might be better for him if he didn't."

"How could you say that?" I asked. I could feel my lower lip trembling.

"Look," he said. "I could lose my job for telling you this, but like you said, we're old friends." He paused and looked about, and when he was satisfied that everyone was gone except for the two of us, he resumed again. "If he makes it," he said, "we're going to pick him up and he's going to be charged with two counts of murder. The D.A. has already issued the arrest warrant. We didn't pick him up today because of the funeral. The chief thought that would be too disrespectful to the families. But the plan was to take him first thing in the morning. That is, before all of this happened."

"He didn't do this," I said.

I saw T-Baby's eyes narrow. "He did it. Ain't no doubt about it."

I shook my head.

"I know you don't want to believe it," he said, "seeing what Luther once meant to you. But it's true. Luther killed his wife and he killed their kid. The case against him is strong. Real strong."

I had managed not to cry, but now I felt a single tear roll down my cheek. "What's going to happen now?"

"We're going to monitor his progress. If he's lucky, he'll die. If he's not, he'll get better, and we'll arrest him, and he'll die anyway. This is a capital offense. If he's convicted, he will be executed."

I closed my eyes, and at that moment I wished that I had not come back here, and that I was not standing in this spot, and that I was not hearing that which I simply could not bear to hear.

"I'm sorry," T-Baby said. "I wish things were different. But they're not. And I don't know what else to tell you."

I didn't answer. Instead, I closed my eyes and turned my head.

"Well, if you remember anything else, please let me know."

"I will," I said.

T-Baby left and I made my way back across the street. A group of neighbors had gathered in our front yard. Mama was standing on the front porch—most of the neighbors were standing under the large pecan tree. I didn't speak to them and I didn't speak to Mama. I simply went into my bedroom, lay across the bed, and wept.

CHAPTER 20

She and I were naked, and my hand was on her thigh. And we were together in another time, and at another place, and I could feel the passion rising within me, and I looked longingly into her eyes, and she told me that she loved me, and that she would forever love me, and I turned to kiss her, but before I could, she was gone. And in that instant, I felt my heart sink again, and I wondered why this was happening to me—and why the place I thought she and I would occupy once I pulled the trigger was still eluding me.

Suddenly the darkness, which had been my home, began to move and in its place was a state of consciousness within which I had existed my entire life. And I felt myself moving farther away from her, and I wanted to grab on to something and hold myself steady until the force of the rolling tide had released me from its grip and ceased to drag me back into a place where I no longer wanted to reside. I was fighting that force when I again found myself becoming aware of my surroundings, and in that moment of consciousness, I could feel the cold, dry air on my badly chafed skin. I could smell the intoxicating scent of my stale, sterilized surroundings. And I could hear the sound of two voices emanating from the corridors just outside my room.

"He was extremely lucky," I heard a man say. "The bullet struck a bone and ricocheted out without doing much damage."

"So, he's going to make it?" I heard my aunt question him.

"Yes," the man said. "His skull was fractured and he suffered some blood loss, but other than that, he should be fine. Thank God he shot himself with a .22; otherwise, he most certainly would not have survived."

And suddenly I heard an unfamiliar voice from some faraway place say, *And in the end, they shall long to die and can't.* And in the next instant my eyes opened, and I was lying on my back, staring at the ceiling, and there was a large bandage around my head, and my vision was blurred, and I turned my head toward the sound of the voices, and I saw my aunt and a strange white man standing just beyond the entrance of my hospital room. I turned my head to look away and the movement, although slight, awakened a sleeping nerve and in an instant I was aware of the sharp, piercing pain in the center of my head. I moaned, and when I did, I saw my aunt's head turn toward me.

"Luther," she called to me.

I slowly turned my head to face her.

"Honey, are you okay?"

I nodded my head, and instantly she clasped her hands over her mouth and I did not know if she was praying or crying. Then I saw the doctor move closer to the bed and as he approached, I looked around. This was no ordinary hospital room. There were no windows and no bathroom, and beyond the room there was a large nurses' station. And there was only one bed in my room, and I was hooked up to several machines. Suddenly I was confused.

"Where am I?" I asked.

"You're in the intensive care unit," the doctor said. "Do you remember what happened?"

I slowly reached up and touched the bandages on my head. Yes, I remembered, and because I did, I closed my eyes in shame. I had tried to go to her, and even in that, I had failed.

"How do you feel?" he asked me.

I did not answer.

"Are you in pain?" he asked.

I looked at him, but still, I did not answer.

"Luther," I heard my aunt call to me, "can you talk?"

I felt drowsy. My head was throbbing, and the room was spinning. I looked at her, then swallowed. I felt the moist saliva ease off the back of my tongue and down my dry, scratchy throat. I winced, then closed my eyes.

"Water," I mumbled.

I was weak and my words came slowly and with some difficulty. I could hear myself clearly. I was speaking barely above a whisper.

"What's wrong with him, Doctor?" I heard my aunt ask.

"His throat is probably a little sore," the doctor said. "We had to intubate him." I felt the doctor's hand on the side of my face, and then he bent over me and inserted something into my ear.

"Are you in any pain?" he asked, again.

"Head hurts," I said, and then I squinted, hoping to still the throbbing sensation pulsating in the center of my brow.

"That's to be expected," he said. "The nurse will give you something for that. Okay?"

He paused and waited for me to answer, and I closed my eyes again, then nodded.

"Are you experiencing any other pain?"

I heard his question, and I felt myself struggling to make my mouth move. Then, I felt my lips part and I heard myself mumble, "Feel drowsy."

"That's the effect of the anesthesia. It should wear off in an hour or two." Then he looked inside my mouth and he shone a tiny flashlight in my eyes. "Everything looks good. We will monitor you tonight and we should be able to move you into a room in the morning. Do you have any other questions?"

I shook my head. Then I saw him turn to my aunt.

"He needs to rest," he said. "You're welcome to sit with him for a little while but visiting hours will end in fifteen minutes. You can sit in the waiting room if you like, but you won't be able to see him again until tomorrow morning."

"What time tomorrow?"

"Seven-thirty," he said. "But I hope to have him in a regular room by eight, and if that's the case, you will be able to sit with him as long as you like. Visiting hours on the floors aren't as re-strictive as they are here on ICU. He paused again. "Do you have any questions?"

"No, sir," she said.

"Well, I will see you in the morning."

"Thank you, Doctor."

The doctor left and my aunt eased back into the room. She was hurting—I could tell by the strained look on her face. She wanted to know why. After all she had done for me, why would I hurt her like this? But she would not ask. At least not now, and I would not offer an explanation. What could I say, anyway? How could I make her understand that her love, as bountiful as it was, was still not enough to sustain me? I needed my family.

I saw her pull a chair next to the bed, and I felt her take my hand in her hand, and I turned to her to speak, but she inter-rupted me.

"Rest, child," she said.

"Water," I mumbled softly.

I saw my aunt rise and remove the small pitcher from the tray. Then, I heard her pour the water, and I saw her lift the tiny Styrofoam cup before me and position the straw next to my mouth. My lips parted, then clasped the straw, and I drank.

CHAPTER 21

There were throngs of people milling about the streets just beyond my window. And though I could hear the soft murmur of their collective voices, the images of their gaunt faces escaped me. For I was haunted not by the image of them or by the image of what I had seen in the house at which I was sure they were staring. The invisible demon tormenting me, as I lay upon the bed in the dark solitude of my room, came not in the fleshly form of some demented spirit, but in the surreal guise of a loaded question. *Why had Luther tried to kill himself?*

I was struggling with that question when I heard the frantic knock upon the front door, and I was surprised when I pulled the curtain back to see Daphne standing on the stoop. She apologized for stopping by so late and explained that she had been stranded at the hospital without her car until Skeeter graciously brought her back to retrieve it. I invited her in, but not before the commotion had awakened my mother. So, the three of us went into the kitchen and when we were all seated around the tiny table, I poured each of us a cup of coffee.

"How is he?" I asked her.

"The doctor said he's going to be fine," she said.

"Well, thank God for that," Mama said.

"I been thanking God all the way over here," Daphne said. "And now I want to thank you." She turned and looked at me and I saw her eyes begin to tear. "I panicked when I saw Luther lying there, bleeding. And I don't know what would have happened if you hadn't done what you did, and I thank you for that."

"I'm just glad he's okay," I said, and I raised the cup to my mouth and took a sip of the coffee. It was still kind of hot and I paused as the hot liquid passed over my tongue and rolled down the back of my throat. I loved Luther, and she knew I loved him. Thus, there was no need to thank me. No need at all.

Who is with him now?" Mother asked.

I saw Daphne shake her head. "Nobody," she said. "He can't have overnight visitors while he is in the intensive care unit."

"Didn't know that's where they had him."

"That's where they got him," Daphne said. "The doctor said they are going to watch him tonight and if everything goes well, they'll put him in a room first thing in the morning. "I'll be there before seven. I pray to God that they will have him in a room by then."

"Well, I will keep him in my prayers, too," Mama said.

Then there was silence.

"Mind if I go with you?" I asked, timidly. "I would like to see him, if it's all right."

I saw Mama look at me and frown angrily. She did not speak, but Daphne did.

"Of course I don't mind," she said. "Might do Luther some good to see you. Might help pull him out of this stupor. Don't know what it's gone take. But the Lord knows, I've done all I know to do."

"Gone take time," Mama said. "He's grieving." And when she said that, she looked at me again. And I knew she was reminding me that Luther was a married man whose wife had just been murdered, and it was not proper for me, his ex-girlfriend, to go to his side in such a public way.

"I been thinking about sending him away for a little while," Daphne said. "I got a little money in the bank. Ain't much. But it's enough to get him to Memphis. I got a sister out there and I'm sure she wouldn't mind taking him in for a day or two. What you think, Miss Hattie?"

"That's a fine idea," Mama said, and she looked at me again. "I would imagine he needs the rest, and a change of scenery, more than he needs company."

Then I saw Daphne's eyes stray again.

"I knew he was taking it hard," she sobbed. "But I never thought he would do something like this." She paused and shook her head. "I never should have left him in that house alone. I should have known better."

"It ain't your fault," Mama said. "You had no way of knowing. Nobody did."

"Sometimes, I wonder why life got to be so hard." She paused for a moment and Mama didn't answer. Neither did I. I looked at Daphne. She had a faraway look in her eyes, and I sensed that she was struggling to find the answer within herself. "I might be wrong for saying it," she began again, "but from where I'm sitting, seem like God ain't seen fit to give Luther nothing but trouble." Her voice broke and she took a sip of coffee and then placed it back on the table. I could tell she was about to cry again.

"It's gone all work out," Mama said. "One way or the other." And though she said that, I knew that her concern was not for Luther, but for me, and I also knew that she felt the turnabout was fair play. Luther, in her way of thinking, was simply reaping what he had sown.

"Yes, ma'am," Daphne said. "I suppose you're right." Then she dabbed her eyes and pushed from the table. "Well, it's late and I better be getting on home. Thank you for the coffee."

"Any time," Mama said. "If you need us," she said, "just let us know."

"I will." She turned to leave but before she could leave, I stopped her.

"Something I need to tell you," I said.

I paused and saw Mama look at me again. Her eyes were telling me to mind my own business, but I couldn't.

"What is it?" Daphne asked, and I could see that she was confused. I paused, again, and though I had turned toward her, I could still feel my mother's eyes on me.

"There's no easy way to say it," I said. "So I'm just going to come straight out with it. Okay?"

"Sounds bad," she said.

"It is," I said—then my mother interrupted me.

"Don't you think we've had enough bad news for one day?" she said. "Whatever you have to say can't wait until tomorrow?"

"No, ma'am," Daphne said. "I would just as soon hear it now, as hear it later." She looked at me and I could see her eyes dim, and I knew that she was bracing herself for what I had to say.

"Well, I'm sorry to be the one to have to tell you," I said, "but I have it on good authority that they're going to arrest Luther, and they're going to charge him with murdering his family."

"Who told you that?" Daphne's voice rose.

"I shouldn't say," I said.

"Please," she said.

I hesitated. I heard my mother sigh.

"T-Baby," I said. "He asked me not to say anything. But you got a right to know."

She closed her eyes and exhaled hard.

"You sure he said that?"

"I'm sure," I said.

"Did he say when?" she asked.

"Just as soon as they know Luther's going to make it."

"Lord! Lord! Lord!" she said. "I just don't know how much more of this I can stand."

"He's going to need a lawyer," I said.

"He can't afford one."

"Well he's going to need one, anyway," I said. "Otherwise, he's going to prison."

"Lord, Lord, Lord," she said again, and I saw the tears streaming down her face. "He just can't afford no lawyer." I saw her hands trembling. She didn't say anything else for a moment. Then I saw her eyes stray and I could tell she was thinking about something else. "I just don't know how anyone could possibly think that he would hurt Juanita or that child."

We remained silent. I saw Daphne shake her head and her broken voice became a tormented whisper. "I just can't understand this," she said.

"It is gone be right," Mama said. "Just get some rest. Things will look better in the morning."

Daphne was looking at her, but I could tell she wasn't listening.

"I just don't understand," she said, again.

"I know," Mama said.

"Juanita was a good wife to Luther," Daphne said, and when she did, she had a faraway look in her eyes. "I always admired the way she looked after him and that boy of theirs."

Mama didn't say anything. Neither did I. But I was surprised that she had mentioned Juanita's name in our house, before me. Had she forgotten that Luther had been mine before Juanita took him away from me? She couldn't have forgotten. Could she?

"She was pregnant," Daphne said. "Did you know that?"

"No," Mama said, "I didn't," and she looked at Daphne, then at me. And though she could see the hurt in my eyes, her eyes reflected no sympathy, only the stern admonition *I told you to keep your big mouth shut*.

"She just found out about it a few days ago," Daphne said. "She had given Luther a son, and now she was hoping to give him a little girl." She paused, and I saw her stare far off into the distance again. "She loved that man so much."

Suddenly, I felt my lips part. "Did he love her?" I heard myself ask, instantly wishing that I could reel my words in before my question registered and she uttered an answer I preferred not to hear.

"He was crazy about her," she said. "And he was crazy about that boy. That's all he ever talked about—his boy and his wife."

"That's nice," I said, and my mother looked at me and then slowly shook her head, disgusted.

CHAPTER 22

I attempted to sleep but just as I would doze off, either a nurse or an aide would appear to take my temperature, or check my vital signs, or replace an I.V. bag, and when they were done, I would lie upon my back again, longing for sleep that would not come. And in my longing, an intermittent pain would flare, and I would bear down hard against the iron bedrail and silently suffer the torment that I somehow felt was meant for me to endure. As I suffered, I could hear the steady ticking of the clock mounted high upon the distant wall, ushering in time, which for me no longer held meaning. Then, at midnight, there was a shift change, and a new nurse came into my room. She was young—in her early twenties, I would guess—and she had short, blond hair and light blue eyes.

"Do you need anything?" she asked, and I thought her question strange. Here I was, being forced to hang on to a life I no longer wanted to live, and the agent of those whose job it was to keep death at bay was asking me if I needed anything. I nodded.

"Are you in pain?" she asked.

"A little," I said.

Then she clumsily administered a shot of morphine, and I must have fallen asleep, for instantly I found myself in the middle of a strange dream. I was lying upon a mattress in a vast sea, and I felt myself drifting effortlessly toward a glowing mass of bright white light. The nearer I drew to the light, the lighter I felt. For there was in me the feeling that I had separated into two distinct entities, one of which was drifting aimlessly on the vast, open sea, and the other was being pulled by a powerful yet invisible force toward the brightness of the light.

And suddenly, I was overcome by a joy, the depth and scope of which I could not identify. And somehow I sensed that the peace and tranquility which had earlier forsaken me was once again beckoning me onward, and I was relieved, for now there was the real possibility that I could somehow escape the menacing hardships of my dreaded existence and abide once again in the time and place of those whom I loved.

Without warning, a sense of the new had been born in me. And now, I focused on the light and I willed myself onward, and there was no fear in me, only hope and joy and peace, and I wondered as I drifted, What was the cause of this newfound peace—had I overdosed on morphine? Or had my heart suddenly stopped beating? Or had an undetected clot dislodged into my bloodstream and slowly ridden the currents of my warm, pulsating blood until it had become permanently lodged in the recesses of my unsuspecting brain? Or had a kind and gentle God simply seen fit to end my suffering and bring me home as I drifted off to sleep in the sterile, quiet, confines of the intensive care unit?

I did not know, nor did I care. I simply focused on the light and surrendered my all to the guiding force that held me in its soft, gentle embrace, and I was living in that moment when I heard the rattling of keys and the heavy sound of hurried footsteps moving nearer and nearer to me. And I felt myself awaken as if from some heavy haze, and I heard about me the sound of a heavy voice.

"I think this is the room," he said.

I turned my head and looked. It was a policeman, a white policeman.

"Are you Luther Jackson?" he asked me. I nodded. Then I saw him remove a pair of handcuffs from his belt. There was a nurse in the room with me. Her excited eyes became wide.

"What is this?" she asked.

"Please step aside," the officer told her.

"Wait a minute," she said. "What is this all about?"

"He's under arrest."

"For what?"

"Murder," the cop told her.

I saw the nurse's mouth fall open and her face turn a dull shade of red and I felt the officer place the cold steel cuff around my left wrist and then attach it to the frame of the bed, and as he did, I did not react. Nor did I speak. I simply stared straight ahead, and felt no feelings of rage or anger, guilt or shame—only a maniacal desire to be beyond it all, in a place where life and death held little meaning except to mark the distance traveled during a journey whose significance had ceased to be. No, I was neither consumed with fear nor convicted by what others had deemed me; I only sought a speedy conclusion to the torment I now knew to be my life. After all, what could they take from me that I had not already lost?

"You have the right to remain silent," the policeman said. "If you give up that right, anything you say can and will be used against you in a court of law. You have the right to an attorney. If you cannot afford an attorney, one will be appointed to you free of charge. Do you understand those rights?"

I nodded, but I did not speak. And I vowed that I would not speak. "Who did he kill?" the nurse asked.

"His wife and kid," the officer said, and I could feel the nurse's eyes on the side of my face. But I did not look at her, nor did I look at the officer. I simply lay on my back, staring straight ahead.

"What's going to happen now?" she said.

"We will guard his room until he is well enough to leave the hospital. When he can leave, we will take him to jail."

In the midst of all of the commotion, a large black orderly transferred me to a mobile bed, and wheeled me through several sets of doors and down two long corridors before placing me in a different room. And as I was being transported, a second police officer walked in front of me, while the officer who had cuffed me to the bed walked beside me. Neither of them spoke to me or to

the orderly. And when they placed me in my room, one officer remained outside while the other stood in the corner, opposite my
bed. The window blinds were open and I could see that dawn's
early light was slowly pushing back the darkness. I looked at the
clock on the wall. It was five A.M.

CHAPTER 23

I rose early to take my bath, and as I soaked, I could hear them out there again. They had gathered on the porch and they were discussing Luther.

"That don't prove nothing," I heard one of them say.

"It proves he crazy," came the voice of another.

"Naw," a different voice rose from amongst them. "That's what he want you to think. He ain't crazy—he just covering his behind. That nigger ain't tried to kill hisself. Hell, he shot hisself with a goddamn cap pistol."

"That's right," another one said. "Whoever heard of trying to kill yourself with a .22?"

"That's what I'm trying to tell you," the first one said. "Nigger just trying to get some sympathy, that's all. Hoping folks will go light on him."

"I don't think Luther would hurt his wife," one of them said. "And I sure as hell don't believe he would hurt that boy of his. That's all that nigger talked about. How much he loved that boy."

"Well, they say they got a pretty good case against him."

"Who say?"

"Peter Boy and Jim."

"How do they know?"

"They say they heard a white man talking at the gas station."

"And?" he asked.

"They say they picked him up this morning."

"I don't believe that."

"That's what they say."

"Well, if white folks said it, I'll be damn if it ain't so."

"I don't know if it's so or not, but I'll be glad when they pick up somebody. This thing got folks scared to come outside."

"Well, I know that's right," another one said. "My wife and some of her lady friends talking about forming a neighborhood watch."

"Neighborhood watch!" I heard one of them say. "Tell 'em they don't need to watch the neighborhood. They just need to watch Luther. Now ya'll can believe what you want, but Luther Jackson killed his wife."

"You don't know that."

"I can't prove it," he said, "but I know it."

"It just doesn't make sense," a woman said. "Why her? Why the child?"

"I'll tell you what I think," he said. "I think they got into it and he accidentally killed his wife. And the child saw it and he killed him to keep him from telling the authorities."

"I can see that," he said.

"Damn right you can see it. Luther Jackson killed his wife. And that's all there is to it."

"I still say Luther wouldn't do something like this."

"One man can't ever say what another man won't do. You never really know what's in a person until something draws it out. How many times you done heard somebody say, I never would have figured old so-and-so would have done that? I'll tell you how many," he said, and then answered his own question. "More times than you can count. Yes, sir. You just never know what's in a man's heart. You just never know."

"Now, that's the truth," one of the others said.

"Maybe he did. Then again, maybe he didn't. I don't know. But I do know him and his old lady were having problems. And when married folks get to acting a fool with each other, anything can happen."

"I don't see it," one of them said.

"Well, if not Luther, then who?"

"Had to be somebody she knew," he said. "Otherwise, why would she open the door?"

"I don't know," he said. "But I done told my wife, until this is over, I don't want her opening that door for nobody but me."

"Ain't no way in hell that woman would have let no stranger in that house that time of night."

"Maybe she didn't let him in," one of them said. "Maybe she left the door unlocked. God knows I'm always on my old lady about locking that door. It don't make no sense but she'll lay up in that house asleep with that door unlocked."

"A woman need to know how to protect herself," another one said. "I done told Mattie I want her to learn how to use that gun. And if anybody gets in on her, I want her to blow his goddamn brains out. No questions asked."

"Luther should have been home," another one said. "A man with a family ain't got no business staying out all night unless he on the job."

"Maybe he was at home," one of them said. "Maybe he did it."

Then suddenly they were interrupted by the shrill sound of a phone ringing, and I heard one of the men say, "Hello." Then a moment later: "What!" And a moment after that: "When?" And later: "Thanks for letting me know. I'll see you when you get home."

There was silence. Then I heard the same man's voice again.

"That was my wife," he said.

"Everything's all right, huh?" one of them asked.

"Yeah," he said. "She just called to tell me that the police just arrested Luther."

"Sho' nuff?" one of them asked.

"That's what she say," he said. "And she ought to know. She works over there."

"I told you," the other one gloated. "Don't ever dispute white folks."

"Well, I'll be damned," I heard another one say.

Then I hurried from the tub and began to towel off. My hands were trembling.

CHAPTER 24

At a quarter to six, a detective entered my room, and he lingered, asking me questions, the answers to which I chose not to supply. Then, at 6:30, a minister came and prayed over me. Fifteen minutes later, a nurse came to empty my bedpan, and shortly after she was done, the doctor stopped by to check my wounds, and through it all, the police officer stood in the corner, carefully watching those who came, ensuring after each had gone that I was still held firmly in place by the steel cuffs binding me to the bed.

And each time he approached the bed, my eyes fell on his gun. And I resolved that when he least expected it, I would remove the gun from his holster and do that which I had failed to do earlier, only this time I would not place the barrel of the gun against the side of my head. Instead, I would shove the barrel deep into my mouth, and when my lips were wrapped around the cold, smooth steel, I would squeeze the trigger and end once and for all my travail in this place that no longer held anything for me.

I was watching, and waiting, when I heard the sound of hurried footsteps in the hall outside my room. I looked toward the door. I heard the officer guarding the door clear his throat. Then I heard him speak.

"May I help you?" he said. Then there was an awkward silence and I knew that whoever was out there was surprised to see the police standing before my door. I closed my eyes again and wished that whoever it was would go away. I did not want to see anyone. I simply wanted the officer to move a little closer so that I could do what I needed to do.

"We're here to see Luther Jackson," I heard a woman say, and instantly I recognized the voice. It was my aunt Daphne. I opened my eyes and looked at the clock high upon the gray concrete wall; it was a little after seven. In a little while she would be perched next to my bed, holding my hand, crying and telling me that we would get through this. No, I did not want to see her. I did not want to see anyone. I turned toward the door. I could hear them clearly.

"I'm sorry," the office said, "but that's just not possible."

"Why not?" Her voice became elevated.

"Ma'am, he's under arrest."

"But I'm his aunt!" she exclaimed.

"I'm sorry, ma'am, but I have my orders. I can't let you see him."

"This is a hospital," she said. "Not a jail. Besides, Luther didn't do this. He's innocent. Please! You have to believe me. He didn't do this."

I listened intently, but for me, her words held no meaning. After all, what did it matter now? Could guilt or innocence change what had been done? Could it make my dead wife breathe again? Could it give me back my son? No, there was nothing she could do. There was nothing anyone could do. I simply wanted her to go away and leave me to the task at hand. I looked at the officer again. He was no longer looking at me. In my mind, I willed him closer. But he did not move. Instead, he stood stone still, staring at the door, listening to the conversation rising up from the halls.

"Ma'am, that's for the courts to decide," the officer said. "Not me."

"No!" I heard the voice speaking to me again. It had been decided. There was no need for courts, and lawyers, and jurors, and judges. Those things were for other men. Not me. My fate had been sealed. My destiny predetermined. Yes, I would go to her, the wife whom I loved, and I would go to him, the son whom I adored, and I would leave the things of this world to those who still craved life.

"Help me, Master," I heard my aunt say.

"Ma'am, I'm going to have to ask you to leave."

"I need to talk to him," my aunt pleaded. "Please, sir, in the name of Jesus. Just let me talk to him."

"I'm sorry, ma'am," he said, "but I can't let you do that."

"But I'm his aunt," she reiterated her earlier point.

"I'm sorry," the officer said. "There's nothing I can do."

I relaxed, convinced now that she would be turned away. Then, in the distance, I heard the sound of another call to my aunt, and as I listened, I realized that it was the feeble voice of my mother-in-law.

"Daphne!" she called.

"Marilyn!" my aunt greeted her.

"They say he killed her," I heard my mother-in-law say. Instantly, I knew that the news of my arrest had traveled beyond the hospital corridors. And she, like the others, would come to gaze into the eyes of him that they said had done the unthinkable. "Is it true?" she asked. "I just don't know what to make of this. Why would he kill her? Why?"

"He ain't killed nobody," I heard my aunt say.

"He told you that?"

"He didn't have to."

"I want to see him," my mother-in-law said.

"No," the officer said.

"But she was my daughter," she gasped. Then her voice broke and I could hear her sobbing openly. Then I heard someone sigh deeply and I heard the officer's voice again.

"Please," he said, "I'm going to have to ask you all to leave. Please go home and let the police handle this."

"Not until I see him," I heard my mother-in-law say. "She was my daughter, and I won't take no for an answer."

"Why don't you let us see him?" my aunt said.

"Please," the officer said. "Do as I ask."

Instantly, I pulled against the cuff binding me to the bed. Why was this happening? Why? Out of the corner of my eye, I saw the officer ease toward the door. Why didn't they just leave? I wanted to scream out to them. I wanted to tell them to go. But I did not. Instead, I waited, feeling the tightness of the cold steel cuff about my frail, limp wrist.

"Let 'em come in," the officer advised.

I swallowed, and though I remained silent, inside I heard myself screaming, *Noooo!*

"Are you sure?" I heard the officer ask.

"I'm sure," his colleague said.

"You got ten minutes," I heard the officer tell them. "That's all."

My aunt entered the room first. She approached the bed slowly, looking first at me, then at the cuff, then back at me.

"Are you all right?" she asked.

I looked away. I would not talk to them. I wouldn't. Suddenly, I heard the sound of my mother-in-law's voice.

"Tell me it ain't so," she said. Her voice was soft, pained, broken. "Tell me you didn't kill my child."

I looked at her. She was standing near the foot of my bed and her husband was standing next to her, and she was holding a white handkerchief in her trembling right hand. And I could tell that in her was the belief that I had done what she and her husband prayed I had not. And in that instant, I wondered how could this lady whom I had known for much of my adult life believe for one second that I would harm those whom I had vowed to protect? And how could she look at me with the eyes of a stranger when she had sat in my house, at my table, and broken bread with me? And how could she doubt my love for her daughter, when she had witnessed it firsthand, and not in a fleeting moment, but through good times and bad, for nearly fifteen years? I looked away from her. I would not answer her, nor would I answer any of them. Let them believe whatever they chose to believe—it no longer mattered to me.

"How could you think such a thing?" I heard my aunt say.

"I don't want to believe it," she said. "God knows, I don't. But the police say he killed them."

"Well, the police is wrong," Daphne said.

"Son," my father-in-law said, "if y'all were having problems, why didn't you come to us?" His voice was trembling.

"This is ridiculous," Daphne said. "He ain't killed nobody. It's just a mistake. A big misunderstanding."

"They said they have new information," Mrs. Miller said.

"Who?"

"The police."

"Well, they're lying," my aunt said.

I saw the officer fidgeting in the corner. I could tell that he did not like what Daphne had said.

"I don't know," my mother-in-law said, weeping. "I just don't know what to believe."

"I don't care what you believe," Daphne said. "But you know as well as I do that this boy didn't do what they said he did. Then she turned me. "Tell her, Luther. Tell her you didn't have anything to do with this."

I didn't say anything. This was well beyond me now. I stared into space, longing for them to leave and for the officer in the corner to move a little closer.

"Go on," she said. "Tell 'em."

"Maybe he shouldn't say anything," I heard a strange voice say. "Not without a lawyer present."

I turned and watched Felicia move next to my aunt. Suddenly, hot shame swept over me. I did not look at her. I couldn't. In the midst of my silence, I saw the policeman look at his watch.

"A few more minutes," he said.

Yes, I said to myself. Please make them leave. My fingers were going numb. I pulled against the cuff and the bed rattled. I grimaced.

"Are you in pain?" Felicia asked, tenderly.

I didn't answer. I saw my mother-in-law looking at her.

"And who are you?" said Mrs. Miller. It had been a long time ago and she did not remember her. There was silence and I saw the two women taking each other in.

"A friend," Felicia finally said.

"What kind of friend?" my mother-in-law asked.

"An old friend," Felicia said.

I saw my mother-in-law squint and I knew she was trying to figure out who she was and why she was here. I was her daughter's husband, and I was the father of her grandchild. So, who was this strange woman standing in the place that only her daughter should occupy?

"You don't belong here," Mrs. Miller said.

"I told her she could come," Daphne said.

I grimaced again. My aunt whirled and looked at the officer.

"Those things are too tight," she said.

"Nothing I can do about that, ma'am," he responded.

"You can remove them," she said. "He's sick. He needs his rest. Why don't you show him some mercy?"

"He's under arrest, ma'am," the officer said. "I'm just following regulations. I'm just doing my job."

"How long are you going to keep those things on him?"

"Until we transport him to the jail."

"When will that be?"

"That's up to the doctors."

"What about bail?" Felicia asked.

"That's up to the judge," he said.

"You mean they're going to let him out?" my mother-in-law said.

"I don't know, ma'am," the officer said. "He has to be arraigned first."

"But it's possible?" she said.

"Possible," he said. "But not probable. He's accused of murder. I doubt that the judge will set bail."

"When will he be arraigned?" Felicia asked.

"As soon as the doctor releases him."

Mr. Miller had been standing near the foot of the bed, struggling to maintain his composure. I glanced at him. Our eyes met.

"We trusted you," he said. "You didn't have to kill her."

My aunt whirled and looked at him. "He didn't kill anybody," she said.

"Time's up," the officer yelled.

I felt my aunt's hand on mine. "We're going to get you out of here," she said. "Don't you worry about that, you hear?"

I did not answer.

"Everybody out," I heard the officer say.

"I'll be back," I heard my aunt say.

"No," the officer said. "This is it. I made an exception today but I won't do it again. No one is allowed in this room. No one except medical personnel, and that's final."

CHAPTER 25

Daphne and I hurried into the parking lot and made our way to the car. As we walked, covering large stretches of concrete in long, hurried strides, my mind raced frantically, searching for a course of action that would ameliorate Luther's situation. I tried to think. But I couldn't. My frazzled mind quickly considered one possibility, then another, rejecting all as soon as I had thought of them. Next to me, Daphne was quiet, contemplative. I wondered what was she thinking. Yes, I would speak to her, and the two of us would put our heads together and devise a plan that would render this terrible nightmare mute.

I was about to open my mouth and speak my plan into existence when I saw her lips part, and I heard her speak for the first time since being expelled from Luther's room.

"Ain't enough, he done lost his family," she said, her words keeping time with the pounding of her feet. "Now they got to put him through this. Got him chained to the bed like some kind of animal. It ain't right," she said. "It just ain't right."

I looked at her but she wasn't looking at me, nor was she speaking to me. She wasn't speaking to anyone. She was thinking aloud. I digested her words and the images they created and formulated thoughts of my own.

"Wish I knew what they had against him," I said, casting out words as a lone fisherman cast out his net, hoping to snag something of value, something that would point me in the proper direction. I paused and looked at her. She was clutching her purse. Her brow was furrowed.

"Don't have nothing," Daphne said. Then she set her purse on the hood of the car and began looking for her keys. Instinct told me to recoil, but logic urged me to press her.

"Have to have something," I said. "Otherwise they wouldn't have arrested him."

She looked up for a moment, and her tacit stare became terse. "Pack of lies," she said. "That's all they got, a big pack of lies."

Anger made her cease speaking. In the distance, I saw Mrs. Miller slowly climbing into the long beige Cadillac her husband had parked underneath the tree just east of the entrance to the hospital. Her husband held her door open until she was seated, then climbed in and slowly drove away. I was watching them when Daphne spoke again.

"Got to be something we can do," she said, "other than just sitting around waiting on them to railroad him."

Again, I contemplated her words. Conjecture swelled within me. I opened my mouth and spoke again.

"Mrs. Miller said the police had some new information. Do you have any idea what she was talking about?"

"Ain't got a clue," she said.

I heard the keys jingle. Then I saw her open the door and slide under the wheel. I climbed in next to her and began fumbling with the seat belt. I hesitated again, my mind swirling.

"Luther ever hit her?" I asked.

She paused, confused.

"Once," she said. "A long time ago."

"Do the police know?"

"They know," she said. "Juanita called them."

Could that be it? Had they uncovered some incriminating act or some minuscule indiscretion that served to demonstrate a remote yet incendiary culpability that proved him capable of homicidal violence?

Was he capable? Could he kill? I pushed the thought far from me. Yet it lingered, ominously, forecasting events I could not conceive.

"That's not good," I said.

"It was a long time ago."

"Doesn't matter," I said. "It's on his record."

She became quiet. I watched her guide the car out of the parking lot and onto the highway. I could tell she was thinking about what I had just said. I could tell she was worried.

"What happened?" I asked.

She hesitated before answering. Her eyes became glazed, and I could tell she was remembering. "She left him," she said. Her voice had become solemn.

"Juanita?"

"Yeah," she said. "And she took the baby."

"Why?" I asked. Instinct told me that this was bad, really bad.

"They'd had an argument."

"Over what?"

"I don't remember," she said. "Just remember it wasn't about much of anything. They were young. They hadn't been married but a year or so, and they were still trying to figure out how to live together."

"How old was the baby?"

"Three or four months."

"Do you remember what happened?"

"Seems like she called Luther at work and told him that the baby needed some milk or something like that. He told her not to call him on the job, and she got mad. Then he asked her where she was, and she told him that she was staying with her girlfriend, Lois. Luther got mad about that."

"Why?"

"Lois was all right. But her friends weren't. To be honest, most of them were a bunch of humbuggish guys who hung out over there, smoking weed and drinking beer."

"I see," I said.

"Well, Luther told her to get his child away from over there. She say she was grown and she told him not to tell her what to do.

And he told her she could do whatever she wanted to but he was coming to get his child. And he walked off his job to go over there."

"Didn't she have money?" I said.

"No, not at the time."

"But I thought she was a teacher."

"She was."

"I don't understand," I said.

"Well, after the baby came, Luther didn't want her to work. He figured she needed to be home with the baby."

"And she didn't agree?"

"I don't think she had a problem with staying home, but she did have a problem with their finances. Luther's job was paying enough for them to get by and nothing else. And Juanita thought it made more sense for her to work and let her mother keep the baby. Well, they argued about it. And they argued about it. And when Luther wouldn't give in, she left."

"Oh," I said, "I see."

"No, I don't think you do," she said. "Luther was real particular about his child."

"That's understandable."

"Well, when I said particular, I meant particular. Luther is my nephew and I took him in and raised him like my own child. And I love him dearly. But after that baby was born, he didn't hardly let anybody come to his house. I mean, we have relatives that Luther wouldn't allow in the house on account that they drank, or smoked, or engaged in a lot of bad talk. He was real particular about that child."

"What about Juanita?"

"She was a good mother. But they were just different. She thought Luther was paranoid and too set in his ways. And he thought she was too careless. And neither one of them would give an inch."

"You think she took the child over there to push Luther's buttons?"

"Maybe," she said. "And maybe not. It's hard to say, but I suspect she went over there because she didn't have anyplace to go."

"Why didn't she go to her mother's house?"

"She did, once or twice."

"You mean, she left more than once?"

"When they first married, look like she'd leave anytime they had a disagreement, she run home to her mama and daddy. Then one day, Marilyn told her she needed to stop all of that running and sit down with her husband and work things out."

"Did she?"

"Eventually, but she turned to her friends first."

"Like Lois?"

"That's right."

"Did Juanita's friend like Luther?"

"Not really. They show him respect. But most of 'em thought he was too strict. Some of them even called him controlling. Whatever that means."

"Was he?"

"No, he was just settled. Juanita was the type of girl who had a lot of friends. When she was at work, she was professional and ladylike, but when she was at home, she liked to visit, and talk loud, and clown around. Luther was just the opposite. He was quiet and private. He was a family man."

"I know," I said, before I realized it. She looked at me and I quickly changed the subject. "So he left his job and went over there, right?"

"No," she said. "He called me first and explained what had happened and asked me to go over there with him to get his child."

"Why?" I asked.

"Just said he didn't want to go over there by himself," she said. "But in my mind, I figured he just didn't want any trouble."

"So what happened?"

"When we got there, the curtains on the bedroom window were open, and we could see the child lying on the bed asleep, and sure enough there was a group of men standing around the room, drinking and smoking.

"Where was Juanita?"

"I don't know. We didn't see her. And to be honest, we didn't look for her. When Luther saw that child he was some angry. I was more concerned with trying to calm him down than anything else."

"Does he have a temper?"

"Not really," she said. "He's quiet. And like a lot of quiet folks he holds things in. And when he finally does let it out, he explodes."

"What do you mean, explodes?"

"Loses his temper."

"Does he become violent?"

"No," she said. "Not violent. He just raises his voice. That's all."

"So, is that what happened?"

"Not really. Like I said, he was going to get his child and leave. But when he went to the front door, Juanita opened the door and blocked it."

"She wouldn't let him in?"

"No, she told him to leave. And he said not without his child. So, he tried to squeeze by her and when he did, she pushed him. And that's when he hit her."

"With his fist?" I asked.

"No, he slapped."

"That's not good," I said.

"I know, and so does he."

"What did she do?"

"Said she was going to call the police. So I pulled him aside and tried to calm him down. He was upset that he had hit her. We left and he called T-Baby and told him what happened. T-Baby came by the house, and after they had talked he told Luther that they had probably issued a warrant for his arrest and that it would probably be better for him if he turned himself in. And that's what he did."

"What happened?"

"They booked him, but they never put him in a cell. They said they appreciated the fact that he turned himself in. But they told him that he should have called them, instead of me, before he went over there. And that under no circumstances is he permitted to hit his wife."

"Did he go to court?"

"He went to court," Daphne said. "He pleaded guilty and the judge sentenced him to community service and he made him attend marriage counseling and anger management classes."

"This is not good," she said. "It's not good at all." What do we do now?"

"Is Benjamin Wilcox still the district attorney?"

"He is," she said.

"Good," I said. He and I were friends in high school." I think we should go see if he will tell us anything."

She nodded, and headed downtown to the D.A.'s office.

CHAPTER 26

I closed my eyes and prayed for sleep, and when it came, my mind kept drifting back to Friday. And I would awaken, only to see the officer standing in the corner, staring at me. He was tired. I looked at the clock. It was after seven. They would relieve him soon. If I were to act, I would have to act before his relief came. Then I thought of something else. My right hand was cuffed and I would have to pull the weapon from his holster with my left hand and fire it before he could react. But what kind of weapon was it? I looked at the gun. Was the safety on or off? I could not tell. Suddenly, I heard the officer speaking to me.

"What are you looking at?" he snapped through tightly clenched teeth. I averted my eyes. What was wrong with me? I had been staring. I needed to be careful unless I arouse his suspicion and foil my plan.

"Keep your eyes off me," he ordered. "You hear?"

I did not answer; instead I stared absently at the wall, giving no indication that I heard him.

"You bastard," he snarled. "You answer me when I talk to you."

He started toward the bed and just as he did, the doctor entered the room, and I could tell by the strained look on the doctor's face that he had heard what had been said. I did not care what had been uttered or what had been done. Words and deeds were beyond me now. I was simply fixed on the gun.

"Is there a problem?" the doctor asked.

The officer looked at me, then back at the doctor. He was angry. I could see it in his eyes.

"No problem," he said.

I saw the doctor look at me, then back at the officer. I could not figure him out. He seemed decent, yet there was something about him that puzzled me. He had spoken to my aunt civilly enough the day before but since my arrest, he had become cold and distant, going about his duties with a detached demeanor that led me to believe that his was an act camouflaged by a professionalism he was obliged to display.

"I need to examine you," the doctor said.

I nodded, and when I did, he approached the bed.

"How are you feeling this morning?" he asked.

"Fine," I said.

"Are you in any pain?"

I shook my head.

Then I felt the doctor's hand on my head. He removed the bandages and examined my wound.

"Do you feel light-headed or dizzy?'

I shook my head again.

He bent at the waist and flipped the switch on the side of the bed. I heard a loud buzz, then suddenly the bed began to move, and when I was in an upright position, he released the button and the bed stopped. Then, without speaking, he removed a tiny flashlight from his pocket and shone it in my eyes. When he was satisfied, he stepped back and raised a single finger on his right hand.

"I want you to follow my finger with your eyes," he said, and I watched him slowly move his finger to his left, reverse himself, and move it back to his right. Then, he turned to the officer.

"I need you to remove the cuffs."

"May I ask why?"

"I need to see him stand and walk," the doctor said.

"Is that necessary?" he asked.

"It's necessary," he said.

The officer approached and I looked at the gun again, then quickly averted my eyes. Was this it? Should I grab the gun now and end this nightmare once and for all or should I wait? And if I waited, would I get a second chance? I sat stone still, weighing my options and feeling the tenseness of the moment as I watched the officer remove the key from his pocket and begin manipulating the cuffs. Suddenly, I became aware of a problem I had not anticipated. There was a thin leather strap holding the gun in the holster. To remove the gun I would have to undo the strap. No, I could not act now. I needed both hands. So, I would wait, and I would feign weakness, and when he was completely off guard, I would snatch the gun from the holster and wrap my lips around the barrel and fire.

"Can you stand?" the doctor asked me.

I clutched the mattress with both hands and slowly turned my body until my legs were dangling over the side. I paused to catch my breath, pretending all along to labor.

"Take your time," the doctor advised.

I hesitated, then eased forward, pressing against the bed with trembling hands. Yes, I had to convince him that I was weak and of no danger to them.

"Easy," the doctor said. "Easy."

I rose to my feet, then wobbled, and instantly, I felt the doctor's hand about my waist.

"Easy," he said, still clutching my waist. "Easy."

I glanced at the gun again. I started to reach for it but the officer was too alert; he was still too cautious.

"Can you walk?" the doctor asked, softly.

"I can try," I said.

He removed his hands from about my waist.

"Now, I want you to walk to the door, turn around, and come back," he said. "Do you think you can do that?"

"I think so," I said.

I took an unsteady step, paused, and resumed my balance, then began again. I saw the doctor watching me.

"He acts like he's drunk," the officer made a crass comment.

"His equilibrium is off," the doctor said.

I feigned unsteadiness and wobbled again.

"Be careful," the doctor cautioned. "Take your time."

I inched closer to the door, and as I did, I could see the officer in the hallway. He had pulled a chair just east of the door and was sitting comfortably. As I approached, he did not stir nor did he look, and I got the distinct impression that he had nodded off.

I reached the door, then turned around and headed back toward the doctor. I wobbled again, then quickly regained my balance before gingerly making my way back to the bed. I collapsed against the bed, breathing heavily and feigning dizziness. I felt the doctor's hands on me again.

"Help me get him back into bed," he told the officer. "He's exhausted."

The officer obliged. I felt him place one hand in the small of my back, and then he bent at the waist, to lift my legs, and when he did, I ripped the thin leather strap loose and grabbed his gun. He whirled, trying to separate me from the gun. I hung on with both hands, my fingers tightly gripping the handle. We struggled, each pulling against the other's weight. We rolled upon the bed; my flailing feet kicked the tray table and it fell to the floor with a thunderous sound. I heard the officer in the hall yell out to his partner. Then behind me, I heard footsteps on the floor. The second officer came running; he drew his nightstick and I felt the sting of his stick slamming hard against the side of my head. I winced and yelled out, but held on as the officer I was fighting with tried to twist the gun out of my hand.

"Turn it a-loose, you son of a bitch!"

I held on, refusing to release my grip. The second officer raised the nightstick and hit me again. I felt the pain shoot through my back.

"Turn it a-loose!" he shouted.

He grabbed the gun with his hand. I bit him, and then I pulled the barrel of the gun toward my mouth.

"Goddammit," he yelled, and I felt him grab me by the back of my collar and yank me from the bed—then I felt the sting of the stick across the back of my legs. My legs buckled and I tumbled forward, landing headlong upon the floor.

"Cuff him."

I heard one officer say something to the other, and instantly I felt his knee in my back, and then I felt my arm being twisted and the steel cuff snapping shut, binding the wrist of my trembling left arm. I screamed out in pain. Then I saw the one whom I had bitten lumber to his feet and reinsert the gun into his holster.

"Cuff both hands," he shouted, his flushed red face livid with fury. "That son of a bitch is crazy."

They lifted me to my feet and flung me roughly upon the bed. And when I was lying supine on my back they cuffed me to the rail. Only this time, they cuffed both hands.

"I don't like this," the doctor said. "He's too violent to be here. He should be in jail."

I looked at the officer. He was breathing heavily.

"Try that again," he said, with hate in his voice. "I'll kill you."

I didn't answer.

"I want him out of here," the doctor said.

"I understand," the officer said. "But he's injured, and according to the law he's entitled to medical attention."

"And my staff is entitled to safety."

"You're in no danger here," he said. "I assure you."

"What if he tries to escape again?"

"He won't."

"Can you guarantee that?"

"I can't guarantee it," he said. "But he's cuffed to the bed and we have him under twenty-four-hour surveillance. That's all we can do."

"That's not good enough," the doctor said. "I want him out of here."

"As soon as he's cleared for discharge."

"He's cleared," the doctor said.

"All right," he said. "But remember one thing—this bastard has rights. If anything happens to him—medically speaking, that is— you're responsible."

"I'll accept that responsibility," he said. "Just get him out."

There was silence.

"I will notify the chief," the officer said.

"When?" the doctor asked.

"Right now," he said. "But I must warn you that the chief is going to want to know his condition. We don't have a medical wing at the jail. If he needs medical attention, the chief is going to insist that he remain here."

"He simply needs rest."

"What about medication?"

"I will prescribe something for his pain."

"I hope you're not overreacting," said the officer.

"Overreacting?" said the doctor. "What if he had gotten that gun? Can you imagine what would have happened?"

"Nothing would have happened," he said.

"How can you say that?"

"There are two of us," he said. "There's nothing he could have done, except gotten himself killed."

CHAPTER 27

It was nearly nine o'clock when the district attorney, Benjamin Wilcox, finally emerged from his office. He had been with a client, a distinguished-looking white man dressed in blue jeans, a white dress shirt, and a pair of shiny brown cowboy boots. The man was carrying a large cowboy hat in his hand, and the district attorney, who followed him out into the reception area, was wearing a dark blue suit, a white shirt, and a red tie. He held a cup in his hand, and I assumed he was drinking coffee. The two of them slowly walked through the reception area and paused just beyond the receptionist's desk.

"I'll take care of that first thing Monday morning," the D.A. said.

"Good enough," the man said.

Then the two of them shook hands and the district attorney affectionately slapped the man on the back.

"Say hello to Meg and the kids for me."

"I will," he said.

The man left and when he did, I rose from the small sofa on which Daphne and I had been sitting and called out to him. "Mr. District Attorney," I said.

"Yes?" he said.

"May I have a word with you?"

He hesitated, then looked at me for a moment.

"Felicia," he said. "Is that you?"

"Yes, sir," I said. "It's me."

He crossed the small room and when he was close, he stopped.

"It's been a long time," he said.

"Too long," I said.

We embraced each other and then he released me and gazed into my eyes. He was still a very handsome man. He stood about six feet tall and weighed about one hundred eighty-five pounds. He had broad shoulders and a thick, muscular chest. His curly black hair was neatly trimmed and his boyish face was set off by a pair of dark brown eyes and a set of clearly defined dimples. In the past, he had always been a kind, honest, opened-minded person. I hoped that was still the case.

"What are you doing back in Brownsville?"

"Visiting my mother."

"How long are you staying?"

"Well, actually, I've moved back."

"Is that right?"

"Yes," I said. "Mother's health is not the best. She's not really able to live alone anymore."

"I understand," he said. "I committed my mother to the local assisted-living facility about a year ago. Our parents have gotten old, and I guess we're getting old, too."

"Isn't that the truth?" I said, and then waited.

He nodded; then smiled, and when I remained quiet, he spoke again.

"Well, what can I do for you this morning?"

"We would like to talk to you about Luther Jackson," I said. "If we could. This is his aunt," I said, "Daphne Gipson."

"Morning, Mrs. Gipson," he said, extending his hand to Daphne. She spoke and shook his hand politely.

Please," he said, "let's go into my office."

We followed him into his office. He took a seat behind his large antique desk. Daphne sat in a chair that had been positioned to the left of his desk, and I sat in a chair directly across from him. He glanced knowingly at me, then leaned back in his chair. Yes, he and I had been close. So had he and Luther, and I sensed he was thinking about that now. He turned his head and looked directly at Daphne. She was sitting tall in her chair, her back straight and her hands folded across her lap. I noticed that her hands were shaking.

"Mrs. Gipson," he said, in a kind, gentle tone. "I am more than willing to speak to you about your nephew. But I want you to know before we get started that I can't get into the specifics of the case. The investigation is still ongoing. Do you understand?"

She nodded. She looked shaken—she *was* shaken. I placed my hand on top of hers to comfort her. I looked at the D.A. He was looking at Daphne.

"I know this is tough on you," he said. "Personally, it's tough for me as well. Luther and I go back a long ways, and I always considered him to be a friend. But professionally, it's not tough at all. No case is ever open-and-shut, but this is about as close as I've ever seen."

"I don't care what you say," she said. "I know my nephew. And I know he wouldn't do anything like that."

"He did it," he said emphatically. "The evidence is irrefutable."

"Why?" she said. "Why would he kill his own family?"

"Ma'am, that speaks to motive," he said, "and I can't get into that."

"Can't?" she said. "Or won't?"

He didn't answer.

"Are you looking at other possibilities?"

I sat back in the chair and looked at him. The question seemed to make him uncomfortable.

"The investigation is still ongoing," he said.

"So is that a yes?" I asked.

"I can't speak to that with any specificity," he said.

"Why not?" I asked.

"I just can't."

"It would help to know what he's up against."

"A mountain of evidence," he said.

"What kind of evidence?"

"I can't get into specifics," he said again.

"He didn't do it," Daphne said, her voice trembling. "Why don't you believe me?"

He didn't answer.

"Can you at least tell me the specific charges against him?"

"He will be charged with three counts of murder in the first degree," he said. He paused and looked directly at me. "His wife was pregnant. Did you know that?"

I nodded, but Daphne remained silent.

"That constitutes special circumstances and it makes this a capital case," he said. "If he is convicted, I will seek the death penalty. I want you to know that."

I swallowed. I felt my hands trembling.

"In this state, capital crimes are unbailable offenses," he said. "So he will be held over in the parish jail until his trial."

"Until his trial?" Daphne shouted.

"Yes, ma'am," he repeated. "Until his trial."

"And how long is that?" she asked.

"I can only guess," he said. "Maybe six months; maybe a year."

"A year!" she exclaimed.

"Yes, ma'am," he said.

"Are you serious?" she asked, shocked.

"Ma'am, it's a distinct possibility."

"Wait a minute," I said. "I'm not a lawyer, but I was under the impression that a defendant was entitled to a speedy trial."

"You're correct," he said. "But in criminal law, bringing a capital murder case to trial within a year would constitute a speedy trial."

"I don't want him setting in jail a year for something he didn't do," Daphne said.

"This is a small town," I said. "It may not take that long, correct?"

"It just depends," he said.

"On what?" I asked.

"On the judge presiding over the case and on the defendant's lawyer. He paused. "Does Luther have a lawyer?"

"Not yet."

He settled back on the chair. "If you want to help him," he said, looking directly at me, "find him a lawyer. A very good lawyer."

"I can't afford a lawyer," Daphne said, returning to her earlier mantra.

"Then one will be appointed by the court."

"No," I said. "I don't want that."

He looked at me, but he didn't say anything. I paused. I had spoken too forcefully. My tone had indicated a proprietory level in Luther's life, which by right I did not have. After a brief moment of silence, I spoke again.

"I know this is highly irregular," I said, "but could you give us the name of a very good attorney?"

"Peter Lawson," he said, without hesitation.

"Lawson," I said. "Never heard of him."

"He works out of Monroe."

"He's good?" I said, indicating my concern.

"He's the best defense lawyer in these parts, bar none. But now I must warn you—he's not cheap. He's not cheap at all."

"But, in your opinion, he's well worth the money?" I said.

"No question about it."

"Do you have his phone number?"

"I'll do one better," he said. "I will give him a call, if you like."

"I would appreciate that," I said.

"Peter's a good man," he said. "And he will do an excellent job for you. Provided he's available."

"When will you know?"

"I will call him this morning and let you know what he has to say." He paused. "Should I have him call you or Mrs. Gipson?"

I looked at Daphne. She nodded at me.

"Very well," he said. "If you will leave your number with the receptionist, I will get that information to you today."

"Thank you," I said.

"Now, regarding the case itself. Once you've hired a lawyer, he will have a right to request discovery, which means he has a right to examine all the evidence we have against Luther. And at that time you will know exactly what you're up against."

"Thank you," I said again.

"Well," he said, "I need to get back to work." He rose to bid us good-bye but before he could, his phone rang.

"The chief on line two," the receptionist said over the intercom.

"Excuse me," he said.

"We'll let you go," I said, rising to leave, but he motioned for us to keep our seats.

"This should only take a minute."

We returned to our seats and he answered his call.

"Chief," he said. Then I heard him say, "He did what?" Then he said, "Did anybody get hurt?" After a moment he asked, "When?" Then I heard him say, "Okay, Chief. Thanks for letting me know."

He placed the phone in the cradle then turned and looked at us. "Luther attacked an officer."

"What!" Daphne shouted.

"It appears that he was attempting to escape."

"Is he all right?" I asked.

"Yes," he said. "So are the officers."

"Thank God for that," I said, wishing that I had thought to inquire about the officers first.

"Where is Luther now?" Daphne asked.

"They're transporting him to the jail."

"When?" I asked.

"Right now."

"Oh my God!" Daphne said.

Then we turned toward the door and left.

CHAPTER 28

The chief of police entered. Six armed officers followed closely. The officers with whom I had struggled stepped forward. One officer's angry eyes were upon me, and on his left arm just below his wrist was a freshly applied bandage. He stretched his arm forward toward the chief.

"Look, Chief," he said. "That bastard bit me."

I saw the chief look at the bandage and then at me.

"You bit my officer?"

I didn't answer.

"Ain't no question about it, Chief," the second officer said. "He's crazy as a lunatic."

"You crazy, son?" the chief asked me.

I didn't answer.

"Get him out of here!" The chief said.

Two of them stepped forward. One chained my feet while another cuffed my hands, and as they did, the others stood observing with weapons drawn, aimed directly at my head, and though I wished to die, the sight of so many guns aimed at me was unnerving.

"We'll take him off your hands now," the chief said to the discharge nurse, who had been quietly standing by.

I felt the hand of one of the officers in the group.

"Move it!" he shouted.

"No!" the nurse interrupted. "He has to be wheeled out of here," she said. "It's hospital policy."

"This bastard can walk," another officer told her.

"He has to be wheeled out," she said again.

"Wheel him out," the chief said.

"No, Chief," he said, stepping away. "This bastard just tried to shoot a cop." He looked at the nurse. "You push him," he said, "because I'll be damned if I will."

She rolled me down the long hall and through the emergency door, and as she did, I was completely surrounded by officers. In the hall, I heard the whispers of shocked observers.

"That's him!"

"What did he do?"

"Killed a bunch of people."

"My God!"

"I hope he rots in hell!"

They rushed me out of the building and into a waiting car. Someone must have told them that I was being transferred to the jail, for there were scores of people standing beyond the hospital in the parking lot, and on the lawn of homes across the street. Yes, the word had spread, and the curious were out, staring, gawking, gossiping.

The distance from the hospital to the parish jail was less than one mile, but after the incident earlier that morning, they were not taking any chances. Now that I had composed myself, there was an impulse in me to do something that would force them to shoot. But what could I do? I was bound, and I was unarmed, and I was completely under their control. Defeated, I slid into the car. T-Baby was driving. He turned and looked at me.

"You better start acting like you got some sense," he warned. "These folks will hurt you! You hear me?"

I did not answer.

He paused and I could see his eyes in the rearview mirror. The blows from the nightstick had bruised my face. My eyes were swollen and my lip was split.

"You all right?" he asked. I could see him looking.

I nodded, but I didn't answer.

"I don't know what's going on inside your head," he said. "But these folks are mad, real mad. That's why the chief came. He wanted to make sure nothing happens to you or to one of his officers."

I looked out of the window. The chief's car was parked on the shoulder directly in front of the car in which I was sitting. Two others were parked directly behind us. After a moment or two, the chief slowly pulled out into the street, his lights flashing. We followed, slowly cruising through the desolate streets, avoiding the main highway, turning left through the parish park, then right along a short throughway. We finally pulled to a stop behind the courthouse and parked next to the small, two-story building which housed the parish jail. As they took me from the car and into the building, I felt nothing, neither fear nor anxiety. Only a calm resolve that for the moment this was where I wanted to be, locked away from the demons who lived beyond the walls, constantly reminding me of all that I had lost and of a life to which I now could never return. Why was this happening to me? My mind was wrestling with that question when a door rattled open and an officer sauntered out.

"Bring him in here," he said.

They took me into a small room, and they fingerprinted me then they took my mug shot, then made me undress. I was searched again, and given an orange jumpsuit with "Brownsville Jail" stamped across the back. When I was dressed, they escorted me through a steel door and into the cell block. As we made our way between the cells, many of the men rose from their bunks and stood before the bars, their hands clenching the steel and their hard, sullen eyes staring at me.

I did not look at them; instead, I stared straight ahead, but even with that, I noticed that some cells held two people, others held only one, and some were completely empty. They led me to the end of the cell block and put me in an empty cell. In the cell to my left was an older gentleman. When I walked pass he was sitting at the small table in the front corner, writing something. I could not tell if it was a letter or some type of journal entry. When I entered, he did not look at me, and I did not look directly at him. I was thankful that he was an older man who seemed accustomed to doing time. I vowed that I would not bother him nor would I allow him to bother me.

When I was inside the cage, and the door clanged shut behind me, there was a brief moment in which I had no idea what to do with myself. So, I climbed uneasily onto the top bunk and stretched out on the mattress, and when I was situated, I looked around. Yes, the cell was drab and tiny, approximately six by ten. There were two bunks, a toilet, a sink, and nothing else. The walls were made of concrete painted a dull shade of gray. There were no windows; nor was there any natural light or outside ventilation. I turned toward the gray concrete wall and closed my eyes. Yes, this was exactly where I wanted to be, lying in a cell, on a bunk, numb to the world. And as I lay on the bunk, feeling the walls of the tiny cell closing in on me, the old man in the next cell lit a cigarette and I could smell the scent floating on the dense, stale air. I inhaled, and I felt my nostrils flare against the nauseating scent. Then I heard a guy in a distant cell calling my name.

"Luther!" he sang in a hoarse, hushed tone. He paused and waited but I remained quiet.

I did not respond.

"Luther Jackson."

I still did not answer.

"I know you hear me," he said.

"Leave him alone," someone shouted from another cell.

"Mind your own business," he shouted back.

Suddenly, it became quiet.

"Luther," he called to me again.

I still did not answer.

"I'm watching you," he said.

I turned flat onto my back and stared at the ceiling. Who was this person? Why was he bothering me? I started to answer, but thought better of it and I waited. He was silent for a moment, then he spoke again.

"You watch your back," he said, "because if I catch you outside that cell, you're a dead man."

CHAPTER 29

I was anxious, and I was afraid, and though it was not my place, I was concerned that some harm had come to him, and in that vein, I desperately needed to see him, and to be near him, and to hear him say that he was okay. And in my longing to be near him, I willed myself to be calm for fear my emotions would betray me and I would disgrace myself before his aunt and those who could not understand. And in that moment, it was all I could do not to lower my eyes and murmur some quiet thing, some soft, sweet expression that a woman only utters to the one she loves. And I did love him—he had to get clear and free of this thing so I could tell him.

At the jail, Daphne and I were searched by a female officer, and when she was satisfied that we possessed no weapons, she led us through a series of steel doors, down a long, dark corridor, and finally into a visitation room where we would be allowed to see Luther. And while we waited, I stood in the center of the floor and Daphne sat at the small metal table. We each remained quiet until the door opened and the officers brought Luther in.

His face was bruised, and his head was still wrapped as it had been at the hospital a few hours before, only now his gown was gone and in its place was an orange jumpsuit with "Brownsville Jail" written across the back. I wanted to go to him, but again, I held firm, suffering myself to remain still.

He sat down and when the officer departed, Daphne moved next to him.

"Are you all right?" she asked.

He didn't answer; instead, he remained seated on the end of the table with his head down and his chained arms between his legs. I saw her looking at his face. She looked as if she wanted to cry.

"They did that?" she exclaimed.

He remained silent.

And in that moment, I again wanted to go to him, and I gave in to that impulse and moved closer. Then I realized that it wasn't my place, and I stopped, secretly praying for the strength to hold on.

"Are you in pain?" she asked.

He didn't answer.

"Do you need a doctor?"

He slowly raised his head and looked from one of us to the other. His eyes were swollen, so was his lip.

"You shouldn't be here," he said.

"Where else am I going to be?" she asked, and when she did, she reached over and gently placed her hand on his back. He did not move, nor did he acknowledge her touch. He simply looked at the floor and shook his head—then his reddish-brown eyes seemed to tear.

"Anywhere," he mumbled. "Anywhere but here."

"Why did they do this to you?"

"It don't matter," he said.

"What do you mean, it don't matter? They saying you attacked a guard. Is that true?"

I didn't answer.

"What were you trying to do?"

"Go to her," he said.

"Go to who?" Daphne asked.

"Juanita," he said.

Daphne looked at him again. "Juanita's dead," she said.

He raised his head for the first time. His eyes were wide, his face serious. He was staring up at the ceiling, looking at an image that only he could see.

"She was calling me," he said, still staring at the ceiling, only now he was slowly moving his head from side to side.

"She's dead," Daphne said.

Then she looked at him, then at me, then back at him. He lowered his head and stared wide-eyed into Daphne's face.

"So was my son," he said, his voice trailing off into a whisper. Suddenly, he looked up at the ceiling again. "He was calling me, too."

"What are you talking about?" Daphne asked. Then she looked up at the ceiling as if she was trying to see what he was seeing.

"He wanted me to help him."

"Who?"

"My son."

"Luther—" she said, but he interrupted her.

"They were hurting him."

"Who?"

"I don't know," he said.

"When?"

"Just now," he said, and when he did, Daphne raised her hands to her mouth as though she was about to cry. I started to say something, but I stopped myself again. This was family business and I had no right to interfere.

"You mean the other day?" she asked.

"No," he said. "Just now."

"That's crazy," she said. "Luther, can't you see that's crazy?"

"Mama was with them," he said, ignoring her.

"Luther," Daphne said. "Your mama's dead. You know that."

"She could see it all," he said.

"What are you talking about?"

"She told me to fight."

"Luther!" Daphne shouted. But he did not look at her; instead, he looked at me. Suddenly, his eyes widened.

"Juanita," he said. He stretched his hands toward me. The chains rattled. I looked at him, stunned.

"That's Felicia," Daphne said. "Juanita's dead."

"Juanita," he said again.

I remained silent.

"Answer him," Daphne said. "He thinks you're Juanita."

"Yes," I said, my voice trembling.

"I'm sorry," he said.

I didn't answer. I could feel my legs shake.

"I love you," he said, and instantly, I felt lightheaded. Then the room began to spin.

"Luther," his aunt said, "that's Felicia."

"I need you," he said.

I felt my eyes begin to well.

"I have to leave," I said. I turned toward the door.

"Don't leave," he said. "Please don't leave."

The guard opened it and I stepped through.

"I love you," Luther shouted again.

I hurried down the corridor.

"Juanita!" I heard him scream.

I was crying.

CHAPTER 30

She ran from the room, and Daphne moved closer to me. And I pulled against the chains binding me to the table, and I struggled to rise, to follow her, but I could not move. I felt my emotions sink again, and I looked at my aunt. Her eyes were wide and her mouth was open, and then in an instant, I was aware of myself again, and in that moment of awareness, I longed again to be alone.

"You shouldn't be here," I said to my aunt.

"Where else am I going to be?"

"Anywhere," I said. "Anywhere but here."

I saw her staring at my face again.

"Why did they do this to you?" she asked.

"It don't matter," I said.

"What do you mean, it don't matter?"

"Go home," I said.

"Don't give these folks a reason," she said.

"I needed to go to her."

"She's dead."

"It's all my fault," I said.

"Mind what you say."

"I killed them," I said. "Sure as they dead, I'm the one who killed them. And I can't live with that."

I dropped my head again, sobbing.

"What's wrong with you?" she asked. "These folks trying to pin this on you," she said. "Don't you understand that?"

I didn't answer.

"I want you to fight," she said. "Do you understand me?"

I didn't answer.

"Do you want to stay in this place the rest of your life?"

I didn't answer.

"Do you?" she shouted.

"What life?" I said angrily.

"What life!" she repeated. "Luther, this is a capital case. If they convict you of this crime you will be sentenced to death. Don't you understand that?"

"I don't care what they do to me," I said.

"You don't care?"

"I don't care," I said.

"What about me?" she shouted. "Do you care about me?" She paused, and looked at me. "What am I supposed to do when they kill you? Am I supposed to go on like nothing happened?"

I didn't answer.

"Don't I deserve better? Don't you owe me something? And what about your wife? What about your son? How they supposed to feel?"

"Feel!" I said. "They're dead. Or did you forget?"

"I know they're dead," she said. "But are they resting? That's what I want to know."

"Resting!" I said.

"Yes," she said. "How can they rest in peace with you carrying on so?"

I didn't answer.

"You need to get up and fight," she said.

I remained quiet.

"Folks saying you killed your family and you lying around feeling sorry for yourself."

"I did kill them," I said.

"That's a lie," she said. "And you know it."

"I didn't pull the trigger," I said. "But I killed them."

"Stop feeling sorry for yourself," she said. "I'm trying to help you. But you need to help yourself."

"I didn't ask for any help."

"Yes, you did," she said. "You asked when you put that gun to your head."

"I just want to be left alone."

"You think you the only person ever hurt?"

I didn't answer.

"Why don't you get up and fight?"

"For what?" I shouted.

"The truth."

"The truth don't matter," I said.

"The truth always matters."

"I want to be alone."

"I don't care what you want," she said.

"Leave me alone."

"Get up!" she said.

"Leave me alone," I said again.

"Get up!" she said. "Get up and fight."

I remained quiet.

"Maybe it's my fault," she said.

I didn't answer.

"Maybe I babied you too much."

I still didn't answer.

"Don't you care about anybody but yourself?"

I still didn't answer.

"What about your son?" she asked. "Don't you know he look-ing at you right now? What you want him to see? You want him to see a coward?"

She paused again. I remained quiet.

"Get up and fight," she said. "If you won't fight for yourself, fight for that child."

I didn't speak.

"Your papa didn't leave much here for you when he died. But

you can leave something for that child. You can leave him what your papa didn't leave for you. You can leave him a name. Why don't you leave that child a name?"

"He got a name," I said.

"Well, make it good," she said.

"How?" I said. "How am I supposed to do that?"

"Prove that his daddy wasn't no killer."

I became quiet again.

"This old world ain't been good to you," she said. "It ain't been good to you at all. And I realize that. But you got a chance to strike back at it. They say you killed your own child. They say you killed your own wife. And if you don't do something about it, this old world is just gone keep on saying that you wasn't worth the time it took to get rid of you. And if that turn out to be the truth, then my life ain't worth nothing, either, because I helped raise you. And if you did what they say, then I help raise a killer. And I can't live with that. I just can't."

"They gone," I said. "Juanita and Darnell."

"But you're not," she said.

"I wish I was."

"Not before you pay me," she said.

I looked at her, confused.

"You owe me," she said. "You owe me for all the time and love I got invested in you. And I aim for you to pay me."

I remained quiet.

"Fight," she said. "Promise you'll fight."

"I can't," I said.

"Why not?"

"Because it don't matter to me now," I said. "Life don't matter. Nothing don't matter."

"It matters to me," she said.

"Why?" he asked.

"Because I need to know I raised an honorable man," she said. "And not a low-down coward."

CHAPTER 31

Shortly before noon, Benjamin Wilcox called and informed me that Peter Lawson had agreed to meet with us in his office at two P.M. I picked Daphne up at her house around 12:30. Her car was old and unreliable, and she was not comfortable with the idea of driving it all the way to Monroe and back. So, I agreed to drive, and for most of the sixty miles into Monroe, neither one of us spoke. I concentrated on the road while Daphne sat stone still, staring straight ahead.

As far up the highway as you could see were acres and acres of cultivated farmland, but I could tell that Daphne was not aware of the land, or of the moment when I entered the city limits of one small town or exited another. During the entire trip, she glanced at me once or twice, and she sighed a time or two, but she did not speak until I pulled to the curb in front of Mr. Lawson's office on Louisville Avenue.

"I don't know how to thank you for this," she said.

"Let's just hope he can help."

"Do you trust Wilcox?" she asked.

"I trust him," I said.

"Why would he recommend a lawyer to defend a person he's trying to convict?" she asked. "It just doesn't make sense to me. I'm afraid he's trying to railroad Luther."

"He wouldn't do that," I said. "He's honest, and he's fair. I've known him for a long time. So has Luther."

"Have you ever heard of Peter Lawson?"

"No," I said, "I haven't. But if Benjamin recommends him, I feel confident that we're in good hands."

"Let's hope you're right," Daphne said.

Inside, Daphne and I stood against the wall while a sturdy man emerged from his office and made his way toward us. He was in his late thirties or early forties, a middle-aged man with an athletic build. He was wearing a dark blue suit with a red tie, and he looked more like the corporate lawyers I had worked for in California than a small-town defense lawyer. He smiled and greeted us, then shook our hands, and we followed him down a short, plush hall, and into a rather large conference room. He took a seat on one side of the table and Daphne and I sat on the other side directly across from him. He smiled again, and there was something about him that gave one the impression that all would be well.

"So, which one of you is related to the defendant? he asked calmly. Then he looked from one of us to the other.

"I am," Daphne said. "I'm his aunt."

"And you?" he said, looking at me.

"I'm his friend," I said.

"Friend," he said. "Don't you mean ex-girlfriend?"

I looked at him, stunned.

"How did you know that?"

"It's my job to know," he said.

He had been carrying a brown manila folder. He placed it on the table, then looked up. He opened the folder and removed a pen from his shirt pocket, then scribbled something on the pad.

"Well," he said, "I am going to be perfectly honest with you. I spoke to Ben about your nephew's case and I must say it looks pretty bleak."

"I don't care how it looks," Daphne said. "I know my nephew and he's no murderer."

"Has he ever been in trouble before?"

"No, sir," she said.

"Never?" he asked.

"Never!" she said.

He leaned back in his chair and I wondered if he knew that she was lying. I started to say something but thought better of it. I needed him to take this case. No, I needed him to win this case. I needed him to win it so Luther and I could be together.

"What about his wife?"

"Not that I know of."

"Were either one of them involved with drugs?"

"Absolutely not."

"Are you sure?"

"I'm positive."

He paused again, and wrote something on the pad.

"What kind of person is he?"

"Well," Daphne said. "He's a good man."

"Does he have any problems I should know about?"

"What do you mean by that?"

"Any skeletons or bad deeds that would suggest to a jury that at one time or the other he lived outside of the law?"

"He takes a drink every now and then. And sometimes he's a little high-spirited. But that's about it."

"Are you sure?"

"I'm positive."

"Did he ever beat his wife?"

"No, sir," she said. "Absolutely not."

"Did his father ever beat his mother?"

"No," she said. "Not that I know of." She paused. "Now, you do know that his father is dead, don't you?"

"No," he said, "I didn't know that." He paused. "What happened to him?"

"He was killed in a hunting accident."

"And how old was Luther when his father was killed?"

"Sixteen, almost seventeen."

"What kind of relation did they have?"

"It was good."

"Did his father ever beat him?"

"He whipped him a time or two."

"With a belt?"

"Sometimes a belt. Sometimes a switch."

He paused and wrote something else on the pad. "Tell me about Luther's mother."

"She was a deeply religious woman who worked hard and minded her own business."

"Where did she work?"

"At the nursing home."

"In Brownsville?"

"Yes, sir."

"What did she do there?"

"She was an aide."

"A nurse's aide?"

"Yes, sir," she said. "And when I say she worked hard, I mean she worked hard. Especially after she lost her husband."

"I take it she was having financial difficulties?"

"Yes, sir," Daphne said. "After she lost her husband's income, she started having trouble making ends meet. So, Luther started mowing lawns and doing odd jobs to try to help out with the bills."

"How old was he?"

"About sixteen."

"Was he a good worker?"

"Yes, sir," she said. "He was a very good worker. But you don't have to take my word for it. You can ask Mr. Miller. He'll tell you."

"Who is Mr. Miller?"

"His father-in-law."

"How would he know?"

"He gave Luther a job."

"So, Luther knew the family before he married into it?"

"Yes, sir. "

"And he and Mr. Miller had a good relationship?"

"Good!" she said. "Mr. Miller was crazy about Luther. He knew

Luther's daddy had died. So, he treated Luther more like a son than an employee."

"I see," he said.

"Well," Daphne said, "Luther hadn't been working for Mr. Miller more than a month or two when tragedy struck again. Luther's mother died."

"Is that right?"

"Yes, sir," she said. "Mr. Lawson, that boy been dealt a terrible hand every since he been in this life."

"It sure appears that way," Mr. Lawson said.

"It appears that way because it is that way," she said.

Mr. Lawson nodded. Then Daphne continued.

"Well, after she died, Luther inherited the house. But he was too young to live by himself, so I took him in."

"Why you?"

"His mother was my sister."

"I see," he said. Then he wrote something on his pad. "How did Luther take his mother's death?"

"He seemed more confused than anything else. He started keeping to himself more. And he became less sociable. And he started hanging around Mr. Miller's more and more. Look like he was just trying to work himself to death. I don't know if he was trying to make enough money to leave here or what. All I know is he shut down and quit talking to just about everybody except Mr. Miller—and maybe Juanita. From my understanding, she was very encouraging and supportive. Especially after he lost his mother."

"That's when they began to date?"

"Yes, sir."

"How long did they date?"

"A couple of years. After that they fell in love and got married."

"How old were they?"

"Eighteen."

"And her father approved?"

"Very much so. By that time, Luther was like a part of their family and Mr. Miller had helped him in more ways than you can count."

"Can you give me an example?"

"Well, he helped Luther go to trade school."

"Helped him how?"

"He paid for it."

"Interesting," Mr. Lawson said.

"But that's not all," she said. "When Luther graduated, Mr. Miller helped him get the job at Louisiana Machinery."

"Is that right?"

"Yes, sir," she said. "He and the owner were friends."

"OK," he said. "Tell me about their marriage."

"Luther and Juanita?"

"Yes."

"What do you want to do know?"

"What kind of husband was he?"

"He was a good husband," Daphne said. "He worked hard and he took care of his family."

"Did he run around on his wife?"

"Absolutely not."

"Did his wife run around on him?"

"No, sir. Juanita wasn't that kind of person."

"Are you sure?"

"Yes, sir," she said. "I'm positive."

"Earlier you said he never beat his wife, correct?"

"Yes, sir. That's right."

"Did he ever hit her?"

"No, sir."

I looked at her, surprised. He had hit her. Why was she lying? I started to say something but thought better of it.

"Did they argue a lot?"

"Some," she said, "but not a lot."

"About what?"

"I really can't say."

"Who do you think killed Luther's wife and child?"

"I don't know."

"But you do know that in homicides like this one, more often than not, the spouse did it."

"I know," she said. "But Luther didn't kill his family."

"For his sake, I hope you're right," he said.

"I'm right," she said. "Ain't no doubt about that."

I had been quiet but now I decided to speak. "Will you represent him?"

"I'm rather expensive," he said.

"How expensive?" I asked.

"My retainer is ten thousand dollars."

"Ten thousand dollars!" Daphne shouted.

"Yes, ma'am," he said. "Ten thousand dollars."

"Can you defend him?" I asked.

"If he can be defended," he said.

"He can be defended," Daphne said. "Because he didn't do anything."

"Well," he said, smiling. "That's your answer."

I took out my checkbook and wrote him a check for ten thousand dollars. When I was through, I extended my hand across the table. He took the check and placed it in the manila envelope.

"You understand that there are no guarantees," he said. "Don't you?"

"We understand," I said.

Good," he said. "Well, I will familiarize myself with his case and get back to you within a day or two."

CHAPTER 32

There were two of them in the cell with me. I did not know either of them, nor could I see them, but they were there. I could feel them, lying motionless on the bed, staring at me, taunting me, calling to me as if from some distant plane. And I wanted them to leave, and I told them so, but they refused, and I rose to challenge them, to make them flee my presence, and when I did, I felt something come over me, a compulsion which I had not known before. And at that precise moment, I yelled for them to show themselves, but again, they refused, and my smoldering temper flared, and I raced to the bed and grabbed the mattress and slung it across the room, and I grabbed the chair on which the other one sat, and I flung it into the wall. And I heard the inmate in the next cell yell, "What's going on over there?" But I ignored him, and I swung hard into the open air, trying to hit that which I could not see, and I yelled at them again, beseeching them to show themselves, and they laughed, and I knew that they were demons, haunting me for deeds done in my sordid past, and I fell into the wall and cried, longing to be free of them and the burdens of my mind which I could no longer bear.

But they did not leave, nor did they accept my pleas for silence and I backed against the wall and slowly slid to the floor, and I raised my knees to my chest and lowered my head, and I clasped my hands behind my neck, then prayed to God, asking Him to forgive me for all that I had done, and pleading with Him to make the demons flee.

And while I was praying, an officer approached my cell. I did not look at him, but I heard the keys in the lock and I heard the door swing open, and I wanted to leap to my feet and flee the cell and put distance between myself and the demons, but I held firm, knowing that my efforts would be in vain. I was rocking back and forth when I heard the officer ask what was wrong with me. I did not answer. But the demons answered for me—*He's crazy*, I heard one of them say. And they began to laugh again, and their laughter became louder, and I clutched my ears and screamed at them to stop, and I kept screaming and I kept rocking, and I felt the officer's hand on my shoulder snatching me to my feet, and I felt him slam me into the wall, and I heard him say, "Pipe down, Jackson!"

And suddenly, the demons obeyed him, and they became quiet, and I opened my eyes, and though I still could not see them, I felt them still lurking about, waiting for the moment when they would again torment me.

"What's wrong with you?" the officer shouted.

I remained quiet, my eyes wide, looking about for the demons that I was sure were looking out at me.

"Stand up," he said. "Your lawyer is here."

I rose to my feet and faced him.

"Stretch out your hands."

I extended my hands and he cuffed them.

"Now, face the wall," he said.

I faced the wall and he shackled my feet, and when he was done, he lead me from the cell and I walked, zombie-like, back to the visitation room. My aunt was there, and Felicia was there, and so was this strange white man whom I had never seen. And they also were there. They had followed me from the cell, and they were lingering in the room, keeping their distance, leering at me as I sat chained to the table with my head bowed down.

"Luther," she said. "This is your lawyer, Mr. Lawson. He's going to explain what's going to happen. Ain't that right, Mr. Lawson?"

In a daze, I slowly raised my head and tried to focus on the tall white man standing before me, but my weary mind continued to wander. My roused spirit could sense that they had followed me here and I was afraid that they would once again mock me, and in so doing, the urge to rise and fight them would surge again. I clenched my fist in eager anticipation of the battle lurking ominously near me.

"That's right," I heard the stranger say. He paused dramatically, and I sat there feeling frightened, and foolish, and ready, as I looked about, wide-eyed, for those who most certainly were hiding themselves in plain view. Then I heard the lawyer's voice again, sounding strong, refined, distinguished.

"Starting tomorrow," he said, "things will began to move rather quickly, but do not be alarmed. It's just the process—it's cold, and it's sterile, and it can be intimidating."

Tomorrow . . . tomorrow . . . the demons said, emerging from their slumber. Then I heard them laughing—loudly, intensely, ominously. I closed my eyes and raised my hands to my temples, trying to concentrate. The attorney paused, and though my head was bowed, I could tell he was looking at me.

"Are you okay?" he asked.

I nodded, and I could feel myself slowly rocking back and forth, pulling gently against the thin chains binding me to the table. I heard my aunt rise and walk toward me, then I felt her comforting arms about my shoulders, challenging me to hold it together and listen to this man whose paid duty it was to save my life and free me from the cage in which I currently lived. I raised my head and the lawyer continued.

"In the morning," he intoned cautiously, then paused, letting his skillful voice waft gently through the tense atmosphere that my strange behavior had created. "We will go into court and the charges against you will be formally read into the record. At that time you will enter a plea. Do you understand?"

"Yes, sir," I said.

He paused again, and when he was certain that I truly understood, he resumed, methodically explaining the process.

"Now, after you enter your plea, I will begin to push the court to set a date for your preliminary hearing. According to the law, you're entitled to a preliminary hearing within ten days of your arraignment. I will attempt to schedule a date within the next couple of days. That way, we can force the prosecutor to reveal his hand long before he's ready. Do you follow me?"

"Yes, sir," I forced myself to say again.

"What about bail?" my aunt asked.

"I am going to request bail," he said. "And I am also going to petition the court to have the case thrown out completely. But neither will happen."

"But how can you be so sure?" my aunt asked.

"Ma'am, your nephew has been charged with a capital crime," he said. "And he is presumed to be both a flight risk and a danger to society. The court is not going to grant bail. No court would."

"So he's going to have to stay in here until this is over?"

"I'm afraid so," he said.

"And there's nothing we can do?"

"No," he said. "Nothing at all."

"My Lord," she said, then closed her eyes and lowered her head and I knew she wanted to cry. I saw Mr. Lawson look at her and for a moment I thought he was going to say something else to her, but at the last minute he seemed to change his mind. He turned and began speaking to me again.

"Now, Mr. Jackson," he said, his dignified voice suddenly become hard, intimidating. "You gave the police a statement shortly after the murder, correct?"

"Yes, sir," I said.

"And in that statement you answered specific questions concerning the night of the murder. Correct?"

"Yes, sir."

"Well, I certainly wish you had not done that," he said.

"I didn't know," I said.

"Well, I read your statement and there are some things in it that are extremely harmful to this case. He paused and shook his head. Then he looked at me. "I sure as hell wish you hadn't spoken to the police without a lawyer," he said again.

"I just didn't know," I repeated myself.

"Did they Mirandize you prior to questioning you?"

I frowned.

"Mirandize?" I said.

"Did they read you your rights?"

"No, sir," I said.

"Are you sure?"

I nodded again.

"Well, based on that omission, I will challenge the admissibility of that statement in court," he said. "And hope to get it thrown out."

"What are the chances?" my aunt asked.

"Slim to none," he said.

"But they didn't read him his rights."

"Yeah," he said. "That's correct. But more than likely, the court will rule that Mr. Jackson was a witness at that point and not a suspect. Witnesses do not have to be Mirandized."

"My Lord," she said.

I saw Mr. Lawson put on his glasses and remove a document from his briefcase. He examined the document a moment, then looked at me.

"Now, Mr. Jackson, I have gone over some of the facts as you stipulated them in your statement. After careful deliberation, I have drawn several definitive conclusions about you, the most disturbing of which is that you, sir, are a goddamn liar."

"Now, wait just one minute," my aunt said.

But he ignored her.

"Where were you the night of the murder?" he snapped.

"At the hotel."

"What hotel?"

"In Cedar Lake," I said.

"All night?" he asked.

"That's right," I said.

"You're lying."

"Now, wait a minute," Daphne snapped again. "If he said he was at the hotel, then he was at the hotel. He don't lie—I raised him better than that."

"He don't?" Mr. Lawson said, and as he spoke to her, he continued to look at me. But I didn't look at him. I looked beyond him.

"No, sir," she said. "He don't!" And if you don't believe that, then maybe we got the wrong lawyer."

"So, he's an honest person."

"Yes, sir, he is."

"And you'll vouch for that."

"That's right."

"Well," he said, "maybe I do owe him an apology."

"Ain't no maybe to it."

"All right," he said. "But before I apologize I would like to introduce you to someone."

He went to the door and knocked. The guard opened the door and a young black man walked in. He was thirty-one or thirty-two, and he was wearing a polo shirt, a pair of khaki pants, and loafers.

"This is Johnny," he said. "Detective Johnny Ray Gray. I took the liberty of hiring him a few days ago. He will be assisting me on this case."

"Pleased to meet you all," Mr. Gray said.

Daphne and Felicia spoke. I did not.

"Aren't you going to speak, Mr. Jackson?" Mr. Lawson asked, and in his voice was a tone warning me to keep quiet.

"Luther," my aunt said sternly. "Speak to the man!" And when she did, I nodded at Mr. Gray. He nodded back.

"Mr. Jackson," the lawyer spoke to me again. "Do you think I owe you an apology?"

I didn't answer.

"I'll assume that means no," he said. "Is that what it means, Mr. Jackson? Is my assumption correct?"

"I thought you were his lawyer," Daphne said. "Why are you harassing him? Why aren't you trying to help him?"

He didn't answer her. Instead, he continued staring at me.

"You're a liar, Mr. Jackson," he said. "Aren't you?"

"No, sir," I said. "I'm not."

"Okay," my aunt said. "That's it. I want you to leave."

He didn't leave. Instead, he turned to the detective.

"Johnny Ray!"

"Yes, sir."

"Was Mr. Jackson at the hotel the night of the murder?"

"No, sir," he said. "He wasn't."

"What is this?" Daphne said. "Are you working for us? Or are you working for Benjamin Wilcox?"

"Where was he?"

"Natchez, Mississippi," he said.

"Now, wait a minute," Daphne screamed.

"Mr. Gray, are you sure?"

"I'm positive, sir," he said.

"Positive!"

"Yes, sir," he said.

"What is this?" Daphne asked. She was looking at the lawyer. But he continued as if he had not heard her.

"If you don't mind," he said to Johnny Ray, "could you please tell me how you were able to determine his whereabouts?"

"I pulled his cell phone records."

"His cell phone records?"

"Yes, sir."

"Did he make a call that night?"

"No, sir," Johnny Ray said, "he did not."

"Does he have to make a phone call in order to be tracked?"

"No, sir," he said.

"Can you explain that?"

"Well, as long as he has the phone on him, and it is turned on, the towers will track his movements."

"Well, I'll be damned," he said, then he looked at me. "Mr. Jackson, did you know that?"

I didn't answer.

"No," he said. "You didn't know it. And there are a lot of other things you don't know. But let me tell you what *I* know. I know that you are a goddamn liar. And I know that you are in a helluva lot of trouble. And I know that if you don't start telling me the truth, you will be convicted and you will be executed."

CHAPTER 33

I followed detective Gray out of the building and onto the landing, just beyond the door leading into the jail. He paused and removed a cigarette from his pocket and lit it. He took a long drag, then tilted his head back and blew a small trail of smoke high into the air. He knew I was behind him but he did not look at me, nor did he speak. Instead, he stared far into the distance and I could tell that he wasn't looking at anything; he was thinking about what he had just heard in the interrogation room.

"You think Mr. Lawson can help him?" I asked.

He didn't answer immediately. Instead, he took another drag on the cigarette, exhaled again, and then looked at me.

"I don't know if anybody can help him," he said.

"He didn't kill his wife," I said.

"Then why is he lying?"

"Maybe he isn't."

"He's lying," he said. "His records prove it."

"They may prove that his phone was in Natchez," I said. "But it doesn't prove anything else."

He took another drag from the cigarette, then flicked it onto the asphalt. I watched it skid a short distance across the parking lot before rolling to a stop next to one of the parked squad cars. I looked up. He was looking at me.

"Mr. Jackson was in Natchez the night his wife was murdered," he said. "Ain't no doubt about that."

"Even if he was," I said, "what does that prove?"

"It proves that he's not credible," he said. "And it may also prove that he attempted to flee the scene."

"Maybe," I said. "But then again, maybe not."

"Come on, Ms. Fontenot. Why else would he leave his house at ten o'clock at night and drive all the way to Natchez, knowing he had to be at work the next morning? The prosecutor will argue that is evidence of flight."

"He didn't flee," I said. "He returned home."

"The prosecution will argue that criminals often return to the scene of the crime. And that in this case, Mr. Jackson had never killed before. In that regard, he attempted to flee, but before he reached his destination, he panicked. So he returned to the scene of the crime to make sure that the victims were dead and that he had not left any evidence behind that would implicate him."

I remained quiet.

"But unbeknownst to him, he has implicated himself at just about every turn. His witness statement is filled with lies and mis-representations. He has attempted suicide, which the prosecutor will argue proves consciousness of guilt. He has attacked an offi-cer, which the prosecutor will argue demonstrates his violent ten-dencies. He has given a false statement to the police regarding his whereabouts, which the prosecutor will argue proves he's hiding something. At this rate, unless he can prove he didn't do it, his best option will be to plead this thing out, provided the D.A. would even be willing to entertain such a notion. And at this point, I'm not sure he would. Right now, he's holding all the cards."

"Okay," I said. "I know it looks bad."

"No," he said. "It *is* bad. There was no sign of forced entry. Nothing was stolen, including her purse, which was in plain view. A witness heard the two of them arguing less than an hour before the murder. The time of death is estimated to be around ten o'clock at night, which is around the time that he left home. The house reveals evidence of a struggle, but she was not raped or robbed. He lied to create an alibi. And finally, the murdered bodies were burned with gasoline and not only has his gasoline container mysteriously disappeared, but residue from a gasoline spill was found in the floor of his car."

"Okay," I said again. "I understand all of that. But what evidence have you found to clear him?"

"None," he said.

"There has to be something."

"Well," he said, "if there is, I haven't found it. At least, not yet, but to his credit, no murder weapon has been found and there is no physical evidence linking him to the crime."

"Well, that's something."

"It's not enough."

"Then we need to find more?"

"We?" he said.

"Yes," I said. "I would like to help. If you will allow it."

"You're his lady, aren't you?"

"I used to be."

"What happened?" he said. "If you don't mind me asking."

"He started seeing someone else."

"His wife?"

"That's right."

"Well, maybe you should count your lucky stars."

"I don't see it that way."

"You love him?"

"That's personal.'

"My apologies," he said.

There was silence.

"Believable or not," I said, "I've always known him to be an honorable man."

"Honorable!"

"Yes," I said. "Honorable."

"Running around on you is honorable?"

"He didn't run around," I said. "He simply fell in love with someone else. That's all."

"Oh," he said.

"And when he did, he told me."

"Is that right?"

"Yes," I said. "It is."

"Well," he said, "you see an honorable man. But don't be surprised if the rest of the world sees a violent predator who killed his wife and kids."

"I know he's in a lot of trouble," I said. "But that's why you're here. And that's why Mr. Lawson is here. I'm convinced that he is not guilty. Now we just have to prove it."

"Ma'am, I'm an investigator, not a miracle worker. All I can do is shake a few trees and see what falls out."

"I understand," I said. "I just want to help."

"How?" he asked.

"I grew up around here," I said. "I know this town, and I know these people. I could show you around."

"Yes," he said. "You can, provided you're prepared for what we might find."

"I'm prepared," I said.

"Okay," he said. "Let's go to work."

"Where do we start?"

"Show me the way to his house."

CHAPTER 34

The detective left and Felicia followed him, but my aunt and Mr. Lawson remained in the room with me. I was tired, and I had grown weary of the whole process. I simply wanted to go to my cell and rest, but my aunt was looking at me, and her eyes were telling me to stay. No, they were telling me to fight. I shifted my weight in the chair and as I did, Mr. Lawson began to talk again.

"Well, I can't put you on the stand," he said. "Opposing counsel will paint you as a liar. So, I am going to have to figure out some other way to defend you, and the only way that I can do that is if you are forthright with me. Now, Mr. Jackson, I need you to come clean with me," he said. "I need you to tell me everything you know."

I was quiet, so my aunt spoke for me. "What do you need him to tell you?" she asked.

"Everything," he said.

"Luther," she said. " I want you to cooperate with Mr. Lawson, you hear?"

I nodded.

"Okay," Mr. Lawson said. "I need to ask you a couple of questions about your wife. He paused and looked down at the tablet. "According to the statement you gave to the police, nothing was missing. Is that correct?"

"As far as I can tell," I said.

"So, robbery does not seem to be the motive."

"No, sir, " I said. "I guess not."

"She was not sexually assaulted," he said. "So rape does not seem to be the motive, either."

"Thank God for that," Daphne said.

"So this attack on her seems to have been personal."

I became quiet.

"The prosecution is going to argue that she knew her killer."

"How do they know?" Daphne said. "They weren't there."

"They don't," he said. "But the fact that there was no sign of forced entry means that either the door was unlocked or that the perpetrator had a key or that she opened the door to let the killer in." He paused. "Did she normally leave the door open?"

"No, sir," I said. "She didn't."

"So the last person known to be with her while she was alive was you, Mr. Jackson. And to make matters worse, shortly before the estimated time of her death, the two of you were fighting?"

"Arguing," Daphne said.

"No," Mr. Lawson said. "According to the witness, a Mrs. Olivia Washington, the two of you were fighting. She told the police that she heard you threaten her, and that she heard sounds of a struggle."

"She's lying."

"Can you prove that?"

"No sir," I said. "I can't."

"What would be her motive to lie?"

"I don't know," I said.

"Did she have it in for you?"

"No, sir."

"Had the two of you ever had a problem?"

"No, sir."

"How long had you all been neighbors?"

"Over twenty years."

"So, she knows you pretty well?"

"Yes, sir," I said.

"And how would you describe your relationship?"

"Friendly."

"Well, that's a problem," he said. "A tremendous problem."

There was silence.

"Do you know of anyone who would want to hurt your wife?"

I paused a moment, thinking. "No, sir," I said.

"Did she have any enemies?"

"None that I know of."

"Was she involved in any kind of illicit activities?"

"No, sir," I said. "She wasn't."

"Were you?"

I heard my aunt sigh again and I could tell that she didn't like his tone and she did not like his questions.

"No, sir," I said.

"What were you doing in Natchez?"

"Nothing." I said.

"You just went to Natchez for no reason?"

"I was just killing time," I said. "After I left the house, I just started driving, and I ended up on Highway 15. I drove for a couple of hours or so and I turned around and came back to the hotel in Cedar Lake."

"So when you told the police that you drove around for an hour or two, that's what you were talking about?"

"Yes, sir," I said.

"Back to your wife," he said. "What kind of teacher was she?"

"She was a good teacher," I said. "In fact, a few years ago she was the teacher of the year."

"So she was popular."

"Very popular," I said.

"No disgruntled students or colleagues?"

"No, sir," I said. "Not that I know of."

Mr. Lawson had been sitting fairly close to the table. All of a sudden, he leaned back in his chair and folded his arms across his chest.

"Do you have a problem with violence?" he asked, bluntly.

"No," I said. "I don't."

"But you and your wife did argue a lot?"

"Yes sir," I said.

"About money?" he asked.

"Mostly about money."

"So, you all were having financial problems?"

"Yes, sir," I said. "We were."

"You were a mechanic and she was a teacher?"

"Yes, sir."

"So, in some respect, you were living off her," he said. "Is that a fair assessment?"

"No, sir," I said. "I made good money. Between the overtime and the freelance work, I did all right."

"What kind of freelance work?"

"Mostly auto repairs."

"At a shop?"

"No, sir. I either went to the person's home or I worked on their cars in my backyard. I didn't have a shop."

"Did you all have a lot of expenses?"

"Not really," I said. "We remodeled the house."

"But you didn't have a mortgage or anything. I mean, you inherited the house, correct?"

"That's correct."

"Did you have a large car note?"

"No, sir," I said. "Our cars were paid for."

"Then I don't understand," he said. "You all should have had an abundance of money."

"Credit card debt," I said.

"How much debt did you have?"

"I don't know exactly."

Mr. Lawson paused, then raised his hands to his face and rubbed the tiredness out of his eyes. He rose from his seat and began pacing back and forth. I remained seated with my head slightly bowed. My aunt was sitting next to me with her hands folded across her lap. She was tired, and she was worried, and I just wanted this all to be over.

"Mr. Jackson," he said, finally speaking again. "You were over-whelmed by your problems, weren't you?"

"No, sir," I said. "Not really. I was working a lot of overtime, and I figured eventually we would catch up on our bills and things would get better. No, sir. I wasn't overwhelmed at all."

"You told the police that your wife accused you of fooling around, didn't you?"

"Yes, sir, I did."

"Were you?"

"Of course not."

"Is that why she threatened to leave you?"

"Yes, sir," I said. "I guess so."

"Was she serious?"

"Yes, sir," I said. "She was serious."

"How do you know?"

"She had packed some of her things."

"That night?"

"Yes, sir," I said.

"Why that night?"

"I don't know," I said.

I raised my head and my eyes fell on the large white clock mounted high upon the wall. I was tired of answering questions. I simply wanted to go back to my cell and rest. I looked at him pacing back and forth. Suddenly, my mind began to wander, and I just wished that this were all over.

"Didn't you tell the police that she had said that some woman called her?"

"Yes, sir."

"And the woman told her that you were fooling around?"

"Yes, sir."

"Who was that woman?"

"I don't know."

"I think you're lying."

"I'm telling the truth," I said.

"Why would someone tell her that?"

"I don't know."

"What did they have to gain?"

"I don't know," I said.

"Mr. Jackson, were you involved with another woman?"

"No, sir."

"I don't believe you."

"I'm telling the truth."

"You told the police that you didn't have an old girlfriend. But you did have an old girlfriend, and she lives across the street. Isn't that true?"

"Yes, sir." I said. "It's true."

"Why did you lie?" he asked.

I looked at my aunt—she was still sitting, her hands still folded across her lap. Only now her face was one huge, angry frown.

"I didn't want to pull her into this," I said.

"Maybe she had something to do with this."

"No," I said.

"How do you know?"

"I just do."

"Well, who do you think killed your wife and child?"

"I have no idea."

"Why would someone single them out?"

"I don't know."

"Mr. Jackson, I'm going to be honest with you. Your behavior in this matter has me extremely concerned."

"I don't understand what you mean," I said.

"Did you love your wife?"

"Yes, sir."

"You say you loved her, and yet you didn't have any reservations about leaving her alone in her condition. Not once did you call to check on her. You were gone all night. You had a cell phone, and yet, not once did you call. Why not, Mr. Jackson? Please explain to me why not."

"I don't know," I said.

"Weren't you concerned that something might happen?"

I didn't answer. I couldn't.

"Mr. Jackson," he said, "you're in a lot of trouble. I hope you understand that." Then he picked up the yellow pad and the manila folder, and I could see that he was preparing to leave.

"I loved my wife," I said.

"I don't believe you," he said. "And neither will a jury."

"Put me on the stand," I said. "I'll make them understand how much I loved my wife."

"I can't do that," he said. "You are a pathological liar with a volatile temper. Opposing counsel will crucify you."

CHAPTER 35

Gray stood on the front porch and looked through the window, and as I watched him, I knew that I needed him. For he, and he alone, possessed the skills necessary to find the key that would eventually help Luther be free. And I knew that I should feel ashamed for wanting Luther so, but I did not care, for I was filled with the desire of a woman half my age, and somehow, I felt that etched in this tragedy was a silver lining crafted specifically for Luther and me, and I was thinking of Luther when the detective spoke to me.

"Nice house," he said.

"Yes, it is," I said, nodding my head slowly.

"Wish I had the key."

"His aunt has one," I said. "She can let you in."

He cupped his hand over the window and peeped into the living room. After a minute or two, he turned and looked at me.

"Where do you stay?" he asked.

"Over there," I said, pointing across the street.

"And the neighbor who heard them arguing?"

"There," I said, I looked to my right and nodded.

How old is she?" he asked, and he seemed to be mentally measuring the distance from one house to the other.

"Mid-to-late sixties," I said.

"Does she wear a hearing aid?"

I paused, thinking. "I don't know," I said. "I've never noticed."

He had been standing on the porch, but now he had climbed down and was standing in Luther's yard, staring at Miss Olivia's house.

"What can you tell me about her?" he asked me.

"She's a nice old lady," I said. "Just a little nosy."

"Is she honest?"

"Yes," I said. "She's honest."

He looked at the house, then shook his head.

"What?" I said.

"Their houses are relatively close. I don't suspect the D.A. will have any problem establishing the fact that she could have heard them fighting. Especially late at night when the rest of the world was asleep."

I looked from one house to the other, but I did not speak. I was thinking about what he had just said.

"I wonder if she's home."

"Probably," I said. "She's always home."

"What does she do?"

"Nothing," I said. "She's retired."

"From what?"

"She was a cook at the high school years ago."

I saw him looking at her house again.

"Did they get along?"

"Who?"

"Mrs. Washington and Mr. Jackson."

"As far as I know."

"So, there was no feud, or anything that would cause her to lie about Mr. Jackson?"

"No," I said. "At least not that I know of."

"Did you see her the day of the murder?"

"She came out into the street just like everyone else."

"Did she say anything?"

"Not to me," I said. "At least, not then."

"But she did say something later."

"Just that she was afraid to stay by herself. And that she would be glad when the killer was caught."

"Fear will make people do and say some strange things."

I didn't answer.

"Let's see if she will talk to us."

We walked the short distance to her house, and when we were on her porch, I knocked on the door and called to her. She answered the door and she seemed more relaxed than when we had last spoken.

"Hi, Miss Olivia," I said. "How are you this evening?"

"Fine," she said, smiling. "And you?"

"Okay," I said.

"Well, I suspect everything is going to be okay now," she said.

"Why do you say that?" I asked.

"Haven't you heard?" she said, still smiling.

"Heard what?" I said

"They arrested Luther."

"And," I said.

"And that's that," she said, and then she smiled again. "Now maybe things can get back to normal around here."

"Normal?" I said. "I don't think anything will be normal until Luther is free again."

"Free?" she said. "Is that what you came here to talk about?"

"Yes, ma'am," I said. "It is."

Mr. Gray was standing behind me. I turned and introduced him.

"This is Mr. Gray," I said, "and he would like to ask you a couple of questions if you don't mind."

"About what?"

"What happened next door."

"Are you the police?" she asked.

"No, ma'am," he said. "I'm not." I watched her watching him. For her, this thing was settled. There was no need for more questions or more investigation. Her mind was at ease. She could sleep again.

"Well, I already told the police what happened." There was a terseness in her voice, a finality in her tone.

"I know," he said. "But would you mind telling me?"

"Who are you?" she asked.

"I'm a private investigator."

She shook her head and leaned back as if preparing to leave. "I've already talked to one investigator," she said. "I don't see much point in talking to another one."

"Ma'am, the investigator you spoke to worked for the state," he explained. "I work for the defense."

"You mean you trying to get that boy off?"

"He's just trying to find the truth," I said.

"I know the truth," she said. "Luther Jackson killed his family."

"Well, I beg to differ," I said. "I don't think Luther was involved in this at all."

"Then you're saying I'm lying?"

"No, ma'am," he interrupted. "She's not."

"I'm talking to Felicia," she said, looking beyond Mr. Gray. Suddenly he became quiet, and I could see that he was upset with me. But I did not care. My only concern was Luther.

"Did you see Luther kill his wife and child?" I asked.

"No," she said. "But I heard them arguing."

"Arguing with someone and killing them is two different things."

"Well, I don't know what else to tell you," she said.

"Maybe you can start by telling me and everybody else that you don't know what happened over there."

"I've told everybody what I know," she said, and I could sense that she was becoming agitated.

"Ma'am," the detective interrupted again. "Did Mr. Jackson keep strange hours?"

I looked at him, trying to understand the purpose of his question.

"Sometimes," she said.

"How strange?" he asked.

"Sometimes he'd come in at two or three in the morning."

"During the week?" He continued to press her.

"Yes, sir."

"That doesn't mean anything," I said. "We know he was working a lot of overtime. He said that himself."

"Don't nobody work that much overtime," she said. "I wouldn't be surprised if he was out catting around. Just like Juanita said."

"Did he leave town a lot?" the detective asked.

"I don't know where he went," she said. "Just know that he wasn't at home."

"He was working," I said, defending him.

"So you say," she said, and then it was quiet again.

The detective looked at me. His eyes were telling me to keep quiet. I looked away. I could feel myself becoming upset.

"Could you tell me who might know where he spent his time?"

"Buck Earl or Mule Bone."

"Who are they?" the detective asked.

"Couple of men he works with." she said.

"Did they hang around here a lot?" the detective asked.

"No, sir," she said. "Luther didn't allow nobody at that house. Sometimes they would stop by to pick him up, but they never got out of the car. Luther would either be sitting on the porch waiting or they would pull on the side of the road and blow the horn. Then he'd come out."

"Did they stop by during the week or during the weekend?"

"Usually on the weekend."

"Did anybody ever stop by to see Juanita?"

"Her folks, mostly, and every now and then one of the teachers from the school. But for the most part, nobody else."

"Male teachers or female teachers?"

"Female," she said. "Luther didn't allow no men at his house. Especially when he wasn't there."

"Was he a jealous man?"

"I don't know about jealous," she said, "but he was particular."

"Did he and his wife ever go out together?"

"They used to," she said. "Before the baby came."

"Then they stopped?"

"Not completely," she said. "But they did slack off some."

"Did they argue a lot?"

"They argued," she said. "But I don't know what you mean by *a lot*."

"Every day," he said. "Once or twice a week."

"It went in spurts," she said. "Sometimes it looked like they got along all right, and other times it looked like they stayed into it."

"You ever see him hit her?"

"No, sir, I didn't."

"You ever hear him curse her?"

"No, sir, I didn't."

"You ever hear him threaten her?"

"No, sir."

"Did Mr. Jackson seem violent to you?"

"He didn't seem violent," she said. "But I guess he was."

She was quiet for a moment. So were we. I saw the detective look at Luther's house again, and then back at Ms. Washington.

"How long have you known Mr. Jackson?"

"Since he was a child."

"And during that time, was he ever mean to you?"

"No, sir."

"Did you ever have any problems with him?"

"No, sir," she said, "I didn't. But that still don't change what I heard that night."

"Exactly what did you hear that night?" he asked, and then waited.

"I already told the police," she said. "I don't see the point in telling you?"

"Ma'am—"

"Look," she said, "I don't have anything else to say."

"Miss Olivia," I said.

"Felicia, give my regards to Hattie."

"Yes, ma'am," I said. "I will."

I watched her close the door and go back inside. I looked at my watch.

"Well," I said, "we don't have time to catch them at work today. If you like, we can go back to the police station now, and go to

Louisiana Machinery in the morning after Luther has been arraigned."

"Sounds good," he said.

We turned to leave, and just as we did, a group of adolescent
boys darted from behind her house and out into the streets.
Three of them were chasing another. One of them swerved to
avoid me. I fell hard against the car; he tumbled and skidded
across the road. The boy looked up, wide-eyed. Then I saw him
clutching his elbow. The skin had been broken. He was bleeding.

"Why don't you watch where you're going?" the detective said.

"It's all right," I said.

"No, it's not all right," the detective said. Then he looked at the
boy sternly. "Apologize to the lady."

"I'm sorry, ma'am," he said, his voice trembling.

"It's okay," I said again. I moved next to him and I took his
elbow in my hand. "We need to take care of this," I said. "You
wouldn't want it to become infected."

"What's your name?" Gray asked.

"Joshua," he said.

"Joshua what?"

"Joshua Edwards."

"You live around here?" he asked.

"Yes, sir."

"What about the rest of them?" He looked up the street. The
rest of them were still running.

"Yes, sir."

"Where were you going in such a hurry?"

"Nowhere."

"Don't lie to me, boy," he said.

The boy remained quiet.

"Stay right here," I said. "I should have something to clean that
cut. It looks pretty nasty."

"Do you know who lives in that house?" the detective asked,
pointing at Luther's house.

"Yes, sir," he said. "The Jacksons."

"Do you know what happened over there?"

"Yes, sir."

"What can you tell me about it?"

"Nothing," he said.

"I would imagine you fellows are in the streets all times of the night," he said. "You mean you guys didn't see anything?"

"No, sir," he said.

I had a handkerchief in my pocket. I removed it and placed it over his wound. He winced, and I apologized.

"Are you sure?" I said. "Mr. Jackson is a friend of mine."

"We stay away from that house," he said.

"Why is that?" the detective asked.

"Because of Mr. Luther."

"What do you mean?"

"He don't play."

We had been standing in the center of the street. A car was approaching, so we moved to the shoulder directly in front of my mother's house. I was still holding the handkerchief on his elbow.

"Is that right?" the detective said.

"Yes, sir," the boy said. "And his wife don't play, either," he said, then quickly corrected himself. "I mean, she didn't before he killed her."

"He!" The detective said. "Do you know who killed her?"

"Yes sir," he said "Mr. Luther."

"Why do you think he killed her?"

"That's what everybody say."

"No, Joshua," I said, and my voice broke. "Mr. Jackson wouldn't do anything like that. I've known him most of my life. He wouldn't do anything like that. I just wish I knew who did. Then maybe the nightmare would end." I paused. Joshua was staring at me, and I could see that he was feeling sorry for me. No, for the pain he heard in my voice.

"You ever see Mr. Jackson hit his wife?" the detective asked. But Joshua was not looking at him; he was still looking at me.

"No, sir," he said.

"You ever see his wife hit him?"

"No, sir," he said.

"Who mows his yard?"

"He does," Joshua said. "And sometimes his boy."

"When?"

"Every Friday."

"Do you know where he keep his gas can?"

"Yes, sir."

"Where?"

"Behind the house, mostly. But sometimes he keeps it in the back of his car."

"How do you know?"

"I've seen it."

"You've seen it?"

"Yes, sir. We play football in that vacant lot next to his house just about every weekend. You can see the can from the lot. He's got some gardening tools back there, too."

"Well, if any of you fellows hear anything, let me know," I said. "You hear?"

"Yes, sir," he said. "But who are you?" he said to the detective.

"I'm Detective Gray," he said. "Can you remember that?"

"Yes, sir."

"In the future, watch where you're going," he said, "all right?"

"Yes, sir," the boy said. He lowered his eyes then I spoke to the detective.

"Can you make it back to the station on your own?" I asked.

"I can make it," he said.

"Then I will take care of his cut now," I said, "and I will see you at the station in the morning."

"Good enough," he said. Then he got in his car and drove away.

CHAPTER 36

At eight o'clock the following morning, I was escorted into the courtroom by a group of armed officers. My attorney was seated at the table, and my aunt and Felicia were sitting behind the wooden banister that separated the spectators from the participants. There were throngs of people crowded into the tiny courtroom. Some of them were crying, but most of them wore looks of angry disbelief.

When I reached the table, I slouched in my seat next to my attorney, staring straight ahead. Behind me I could hear the soft murmurs of folks as they speculated on my fate and pondered how things could have gotten so far out of hand. Then the judge entered and climbed behind the desk, and at the appropriate time I rose, entered a plea, and then sat down again. The attorneys argued in legalese, and the judge ruled on one matter after another, and when both sides were satisfied, he set a date for the preliminary hearing; it would be two days from now.

And then, as quickly as it had begun, it was over, and I went back to my cell and climbed up on my bunk, and my mind was weary, and I wished that this were all over, and that I could make peace with all that had occurred, and I wanted to give up, but the spirit of my dead son would not let me. So, I forced myself onward. I slept when I could, I rose when commanded, ate, and slept again. I dreamed of happier times, and better places; and I

wished there was something I could do to break the monotony of
my existence. Oh, to have an engine to repair, or a yard to mow, or
a fence to paint—anything to occupy my mind and fill the space
that idle time had created.

Over the next two days, I saw people come and go. A young
boy was arrested for shoplifting. A man was brought in for failure
to pay child support. The guy on the far end tried to commit suicide—somehow he had gotten his hands on a razor blade and he
slit his wrist. The guy in the cell next to me was taken away. Space
had been located for him in Baton Rouge; he was on his way to
Hunts Correctional Facility.

Then the demons returned, and I fought them again. The chief
called the doctor, who placed me on medication, and I slept.

CHAPTER 37

I watched Luther enter the courtroom, and then exit. He looked broken and dejected, and I turned to detective Gray sitting next to me and said that this is not good. Inside my soul, I was stricken with fear that Miss Olivia, a woman whom I had known since childhood, would speak to a jury as she had spoken to me and her words, however misguided, would persuade them to take from me the one whom I now knew I did not want to live without. I was aware of the voice again, telling me that this thing was serious, and I pushed my fears from me and concentrated on the things I must do to help free Luther from this curse, and I hurried from the courtroom, with the detective in tow, and pointed the way to Louisiana Machinery.

Louisiana Machinery was located on the outskirts of town. It was owned by Robert Butler, a local boy who began by repairing small engines and farm equipment, and eventually won a government contract to repair Caterpillars, bulldozers, and the heavy machinery used to build roads and clear land for large construction sites. In that regard, he had made it big. In fact, according to the talk around town, he was a millionaire a few times over.

When we arrived, we spoke to the manager and he pulled the two men we desired to see from the floor and they met us in the large break room. They walked in, both covered with sweat. We shook hands, then the one they called Buck Earl spoke first.

"What can we do for you?" he asked.

"I would like to ask you a couple of questions about Luther Jackson," he said. "I hope you don't mind."

I saw him wipe the sweat from his forehead. The other one, the one they called Mule Bone, was holding a can of soda. He tilted his head back and took a drink.

"You men are friends of his, right?"

"That's right," one of them said.

"My name is Detective Gray," he said, "and this is Mrs. Fontenot. We're trying to help Mr. Jackson with his case and we were hoping that you men could help us out."

"Well, we don't know any more about it than the next fellow," Mule Bone said, "but we're willing to help out if we can."

I appreciate that," Gray said, and then asked his first question. "I understand that you two spent a great deal of time with Mr. Jackson. Is that correct?"

"More than most," Mule Bone said.

"Did he ever talk about his wife?"

"Not much," Mule Bone answered again. Buck Earl shook his head, too, but he did not speak.

"Did he ever say they were having problems?"

"Not really," Mule Bone said.

"What do you mean, *not really*?"

"Well," Mule Bone said, explaining himself, "sometimes Luther would stop by the house and I could tell that him and his old lady had had a round and that he was just trying to let things settle down."

"So it was normal for him to go for a ride when the two of them were having a disagreement?" I said.

"Yeah," he said. "It was."

"Did he ever say what they were fighting about?"

"No, he didn't usually talk his business, and we didn't ask him to."

"Never?" I pressed.

"No," he said. "Oh, sometimes I might crack a joke or something to relieve his stress. But that was about as far as it would go."

"What kind of joke?"

"Oh, I'd say something like it's better to sleep on a rooftop than to live in a house with a brooding woman. And he'd laugh and that would be the end of it."

I looked at him and shook my head.

"Oh, don't look at me like that," he said. "That's scripture."

"That's right," Buck Earl chimed. "Now, no offense," he said, "but ole Mule and me is a little older than Luther. And we both been married a considerable length of time. So we use to take time with him and try to share little pearls of wisdom with him. You know. Let him know that when you dealing with a woman, especially after you and her done married, you can't see everything and you can't hear everything. If you do, you won't ever have no peace."

"Is that right?" the detective said.

"Is that right!" Buck Earl repeated the question, then followed with one of his own. "Mr. Gray, are you married?"

"No," the detective said. "I'm not."

"Do you plan on marrying?"

"Someday, I suppose."

"Well, when you do," Buck Earl said, "you're going to find out that don't nothing make a woman happier than to see a man aggravated. They get a thrill out of it."

I frowned again

"No offense, ma'am," he said again. "But you know I'm telling the truth."

I didn't answer him.

"Does Luther have a temper?" The detective changed the subject.

"Every man has a temper," Mule Bone said.

"I take that to mean yes."

"Well, you can take it however you want to," he said. "Now, I suspect he does, because like I said, every man does. But now, I also have to tell you, I ain't never seen him lose it."

"Me either," Buck Earl said. "And I've seen him in some pretty sticky situations."

"Is he violent?"

"Luther?" he said. "Don't make me laugh."

"Did either of you know he was arrested once?"

I looked at the detective, and he looked at me as if to let me know that he realized that neither Luther nor I had been totally forthcoming with him. And that he had done his homework.

"For what?" Mule Bone asked.

"He slapped his wife."

"Aw, hell, that don't constitute violence in my book. Ain't a person on this planet ain't never hit nobody. I suppose his wife took a poke or two at him. Besides, that was a long time ago and as far as I know, Luther ain't never hit his wife again."

"Did you talk to Luther the night his wife was killed?"

"No, I didn't."

"Me neither."

"What about since?"

"Hadn't seen him."

"Me neither," Buck Earl said again.

"Did he do drugs?"

"Who!"

"Luther."

They both threw their heads back and laughed.

"It's a serious question," the detective said.

"Ain't that serious," Buck Earl said. "Especially if you know Luther."

"Naw, he didn't do no drugs," Mule Bone said. "But he did drink a little."

"Heavy?" the detective asked.

"Naw," Mule Bone said. "I ain't never seen Luther drink more than a beer in one sitting. And he didn't do that very often. More likely to see him sucking on a soda than drinking hard liquor."

"Do you think he killed his family?"

"I can't see it," Mule Bone said. "Not unless something went terribly wrong."

"What do you mean?"

"Any man will kill," he said, "if he's pushed into it. But for a man like Luther who loved his family as much as he did, something got to go terribly wrong. And it's got to catch him off guard."

"Something like what?"

"Well, now, I ain't saying it happened," Mule Bone said, "but in my experience, ain't but two things I could think of that would cause a man like Luther to kill his family. He would either have to catch his ole lady with another man or he would have to find out that she was leaving him. Either way, I could see a man who loved his wife as much as Luther loved his, killing her before he let somebody else have her, or before he tried to live without her hisself."

"Was she fooling around?" the detective asked.

"Naw," Mule Bone said. "Juanita wasn't the kind of woman to run around. But she was on the verge of leaving. At least that's what she had Luther believing."

"Why?" I asked.

"I don't know," he said. "But I tell you what. When you figure that out, you'll solve this riddle."

"You ever know him to go to Natchez?"

They threw their heads back and laughed again.

"What's so funny?"

"That boy practically lived in Natchez."

"Do you have any idea what he was doing over there?"

They laughed again.

"Yeah?" they sang in unison.

"What?" the detective asked.

"Gambling," Buck Earl said.

"How do you know?"

"Ole Mule and me is the ones who got him started."

"Started what?"

"Going to the casinos," he said. "Luther's a regular."

"Yeah," Mule Bone chimed. "That boy took to gambling like a duck take to water. Luther is a homebody. And we were just trying to get the boy out of the house. You know, it ain't good for married folks to sit around one another as much as he was doing. But I never would have figured that boy would go off the deep end."

"And he is in deep," Buck Earl said.

"How deep?" the detective asked.

"Now, this is just between us, ain't it?" Buck Earl asked.

The detective nodded. So did I.

"Well, the way I hear it, he owes the casino about thirty thousand dollars."

"Thirty thousand dollars!" I said.

"That's what I hear."

"From who?" the detective asked.

"My bookie," Buck Earl said, then smiled. "I play the horses, too."

"Is Luther's problem common knowledge?"

"No," he said. "I'd be surprised if more than two or three people around here knew. Luther kept it real quiet. Hell, I wouldn't be surprised if Juanita didn't even know. That's why he went all the way to Natchez. Most folks from around here go to Vicksburg or to Shreveport. He didn't want to run into anybody, so he only gambles in Natchez."

"Which casino does he go to?"

"The Isle of Capri," he said. "It's right there on Silver Street. Just off the Mississippi River Bridge."

"Are you sure about this?"

"I'm positive," he said.

"Lost most of his money playing blackjack," Mule Bone said.

"Is that right?" the detective asked.

"Yes, sir," Mule Bone said again. "That's his albatross."

"We'd been trying to get him into a program," Buck Earl said, "but he never would go. Hell, we never could get him to admit he had a problem. He just kept saying that he just had a run of bad luck."

"Have you told this to anyone else?"

"No, sir," he said. "We haven't."

"Please don't," the detective said. "At least until I've had a chance to talk to Luther."

"We won't," he said.

"You think you can help Luther?"

"I hope so," the detective said.

"Me, too," Mule Bone said.

I saw the other one looking at his watch.

"Well," he said. "We better get on back to work. Boss man don't like for us to stand around too long."

"I understand," I said. "Thank you for your time."

They left and when they were gone, Gray turned to me.

"This goes to motive," he said. "This could be bad. Real bad."

"What do we do now?" I asked.

"Go to Natchez," he said. "To see if this is true."

"And if it is?"

"We have a problem," he said. "A really big problem."

CHAPTER 38

I sat blankly behind the table, watching the well-dressed lawyers argue about evidence, and rules of law, and the admissibility of this, and the relevance of that, or whether a particular line of questioning would be allowed or not. By noon, when much of their haggling had been resolved, they were ready to begin the hearing. The prosecutor went first; I watched him rise and make his way to the center of the court. When he did, his pleasant face became tense, his blue eyes became narrow, and with a rage and contempt he displayed for the case that had brought us all here, he called his first witness.

I heard the name clearly enough: Antonio Johnson. But not until the door swung open and I saw him walk into the courtroom and climb onto the witness stand did I recognize him as the officer they all called A.J.

When he took his seat, he looked at me with eyes made hard by the ugliness of the moment, and in that regard, I knew he was letting me know that he did not like me. And that he would do everything in his power to make sure that I got what I deserved. As he looked out at me, I looked back at him, and as I did, Mr. Lawson reminded me that this was not a trial. It was merely a probable-cause hearing, the explicit intent of which was to determine whether or not there was sufficient evidence to hold me

over for trial. I nodded, assuring him that I understood, all the
while never removing my eyes from the one who refused to remove his eyes from me. I heard A.J. tell the prosecutor that he
was the first officer on the scene, and when he arrived, the defendant was standing near the front porch, the defendant appeared
to be distraught, extremely distraught.

Suddenly, I was home again, and I was standing before them.
My confused eyes were refusing to accept what they were seeing,
and I was frozen in that moment, not knowing what to say, not
knowing what to do, when I heard the prosecutor's voice again.

"Did you have occasion to enter the house?"

"Yes, sir, I did."

"What did you see?"

"Two smoldering bodies lying in the center of the floor."

"The victims?"

"Yes, sir."

"What else did you observe?"

"The strong smell of gasoline."

"In the house?"

"Yes, sir," he said. "The bodies had been soaked in gasoline before being ignited."

"How were the victims killed?"

"They were beaten to death."

Suddenly, I closed my eyes against the image of someone beating my wife and child to death. While my eyes were closed, I
heard my son's voice again. *Daddy* . . . I heard him say. *Help me* . . .
He's hurting me . . . *Please* . . . *Daddy* . . . *help me* . . . My arms grew
tense and my back stiffened, and I felt myself squirming in my
seat. Then, I felt my attorney's hand on my knee.

"Relax," he whispered. "Just relax."

I opened my eyes and looked at the prosecutor. He was holding a yellow pad in his hand. He glanced at the pad, then asked his
next question.

"What else did you observe?"

"The victim's purse was in plain view," the officer said.

"Did you examine it?"

"Yes, sir."

"What did you find?"

"Money, sir."

"How much money?"

"One hundred and fifty dollars."

"Was any other property missing from the house?"

"No, sir."

"So, this was not a robbery?"

"No, sir," he said. "It was not."

"What else did you observe?"

"There was no sign of forced entry," he said. "So either the victim let the perpetrator in or the perpetrator was already inside."

"Would you say that this was a particularly violent crime?"

"Yes, sir," he said.

"Have you had the occasion to observe any violent behavior with regard to this defendant?"

"Yes, sir."

"When?"

"The day we took the defendant into custody."

"At jail?"

"No, sir," he said. "At the hospital."

"What happened?"

"He attacked an officer."

"What do you mean?"

"He attempted to overpower him and take his weapon."

"Have you observed any other acts of violence on the part of the defendant?"

"Yes, sir."

"Please tell the court."

"In a moment of rage," he said, "he ransacked his cell."

He paused, and the prosecutor asked his next question.

"Do you recall the condition of the defendant's house on the morning of the murder?"

"Yes, sir," he said. "It had been ransacked. Especially the kitchen."

"But didn't you testify that the defendant's home had not been burglarized?"

"Yes, sir."

"Then how do you explain the condition of the house?"

"The condition of the defendant's house seems to indicate a violent struggle, not burglary."

"Were you able to confirm that?'

"Yes, sir."

"How?"

"A neighbor heard them fighting."

"Fighting?"

"Yes, sir."

"Did you have occasion to interview the defendant?"

"Yes, sir."

"When?"

"Shortly after we left the crime scene."

"At the time of that interview, was he a suspect?"

"No, sir," the cop said. "He wasn't."

"At any time was he treated as a suspect?"

"No, sir."

"When you transported him to the station, did you cuff him?"

"No, sir."

"Did you place him on the front seat or the back seat?"

"On the front seat, sir."

"Is that customary protocol when transporting a suspect?"

"No, sir," he said.

"How would you normally transport a murder suspect?"

"He would be cuffed and placed on the back seat."

The prosecutor paused, and when he did, Officer Johnson looked at me with eyes of hate. Then I heard the prosecutor's voice again directing the witness back to the beginning of the story.

"Officer Johnson," he said. "Earlier, you stated to the court that you were aware of the strong smell of gasoline on the premises when you arrived, correct?"

"That's correct," he said.

"Did you notice anything else in that regard?"

"Yes," he said. "I did."

"What?"

"I saw a lawn mower, but no gas can," he said.

"Did you ever locate the gas can?"

"No, sir, I did not."

"So, what did you do?"

"I called in the K-9 unit."

"What happened."

"The dog got a hit in the defendant's car."

"What did you discover?"

"Gasoline."

The attorney turned and looked at me, then back at the judge. "Nothing further," he said.

I could tell that the court was riveted by his testimony. He was a cop, and he was credible, and his testimony had been persuasive. I watched the prosecutor take his seat, and then I saw Mr. Lawson rise and approach the witness.

"Did you ever find a murder weapon?" he asked, his first question.

"No, sir," the officer said.

"Did you find any DNA evidence linking Mr. Jackson to this crime?" Mr. Lawson asked.

"No, sir," he said, "I didn't."

"Did you find anyone who actually saw Mr. Jackson kill his wife and child on the night in question?" Mr. Lawson stressed the word *saw*.

"No, sir," the officer said.

"Were you aware that Mr. Jackson mows his own lawn?" Mr. Lawson pressed him.

"Yes, sir," he said. "I was."

"Were you also aware that Mr. Jackson transports the gasoline he uses to fuel his lawn mower in his vehicle?"

"No, sir," he said. "I wasn't."

"Now, Officer Johnson, isn't it possible that Mr. Jackson spilled gasoline in his car while hauling fuel to mow his lawn?"

"Yes, sir," he said. "I guess it's possible."

"Not only possible," he said, "but probable, wouldn't you say?"

"Yes, sir," he said.

"Nothing further," Lawson said.

He turned and walked back toward the table. The courtroom was quiet.

CHAPTER 39

Outside, Gray smoked a cigarette and then he and I got into his car and headed to Natchez. As we did, I was fully aware that I had to be back in Brownsville by early afternoon. To my surprise, I had learned that I was on the witness list for the prosecution and in all likelihood I would be called to testify once the hearing was under way.

We departed Brownsville, traveling south on Highway 17—I was extremely anxious. And though I had not wanted to, I now had to admit that Luther was a troubled soul, and he had monumental problems—and there was the very real possibility that he could have been pushed to do that which I had not believed possible. And there was a yearning inside of me to cease my quest for fear I should find more evidence condemning him to a fate which mentally I could not bear to contemplate.

And in my heightened state of anxiety, the rush of the tires lulled me, and I dozed in and out of consciousness as we passed through one small town after another until we finally navigated the large suspension bridge across the Mississippi River and into Natchez.

The entire trip took less than two hours, and once we arrived, he slowly drove the car onto Canal Street and then onto Silver Street, finally rolling to a stop in the parking lot just beyond the large sign that read ISLE OF CAPRI CASINO. His head was tilted and his eyes were cast outward, gazing with wonderment upon the waters of the mighty Mississippi.

"What now?" I asked.

I startled him. He turned toward me abruptly.

"We go inside," he said, "and we look for anyone who knew Luther." He removed the key from the ignition and placed it in his pocket. I waited for him to say more and when he did not, I spoke again.

"And when we find them," I said, "then what?"

"We ask them if they saw him that night."

"The night of the murder?"

"Yes."

"And if they did?" I said.

"Then we try to determine what time he arrived and how he was behaving."

"How he was behaving?"

"Yes," he said.

"Why do we need to know that?"

"Well, if Mr. Jackson killed his wife and child, as the prosecution contends, and he fled to Natchez, as we now know he did, then his behavior should have reflected something other than the norm."

"Okay," I said. "I see that."

"Now, on the other hand, if Mr. Jackson was playing blackjack and behaving as he normally behaves, then in my mind, that's either evidence of a clear consciences and thus proof of his innocence, or it's proof that he's a psychopath."

"He's no psychopath," I said. "I can assure you of that."

"Well, if he killed his wife and child, and then came over here and played blackjack as if nothing happened, then that's the only explanation that will fly. A jury will have to believe that he's a psychopath."

"And if they don't?"

"Then he goes home."

"This is a huge casino," I said. "Hundreds of people visit it every night. How do you find someone who would happen to remember seeing Luther on that particular night? And who happened to remember his mood?"

"Well, his friends said that he goes to the same casino and he plays the same game, right?"

"Yes," I said. "Blackjack."

"And he loses a lot, right?"

"Yes," I said.

"Then the manager of the hotel will know him," he said, "and so will the blackjack dealer."

We entered the hotel and passed through the lobby, then made our way into the casino. Instantly, I was aware of the festive sounds of the slot machines and the roulette wheels, and I could hear the loud, raucous sound of men laughing and women shouting. Up ahead, I spied a man wearing a red jacket and black trousers.

"He looks like a manager," I said.

We approached him and introduced ourselves. He was new, and he didn't know Luther, but he said if he was a frequent guest of the casino, he knew who would. We followed him through a series of doors and stopped before one marked manager's office. Inside, we found a well-dressed man sitting behind the desk, smoking a rather large cigar.

"Welcome to the Isle of Capri," he said.

We were introduced, and when he was informed of our business, he checked the records and called the blackjack dealer. They talked a moment and he hung up the phone.

"He was here," he said, "but he didn't gamble."

"He didn't?" I said.

"No," he said, and as he talked, he examined the computer screen again. "According to our records, Mr. Jackson checked into a room at 11:45, and he checked out the next morning at four. While he was here, he never went into the casino."

"Which room?"

"Room 222."

"How did he pay for the room?"

"It was complimentary," he said "He's one of our VIPs."

"Did the staff report finding anything unusual in that room?" asked Gray.

"Like what, sir?"

"Blood or the smell of gasoline."

"No," he said. "There's no record of that." The man paused. "Is Mr. Jackson in some kind of trouble?"

"I'm afraid so," he said. "But we're hoping it's just a huge misunderstanding."

There was silence.

"Anything else?" he asked.

"No," Gray said. "You've been a big help. Thank you for your time."

We went outside and when we were near the car, he leaned against the hood and looked out over the river.

"A compulsive gambler checks into the hotel of his favorite casino and spends the night, but he doesn't gamble. How do you explain that?"

"I can't," I said. "Can you?"

"Yes, I believe I can."

"Please do."

"It's simple," he responded. "He was hiding."

CHAPTER 40

I could hear the voices again, swirling about me, seemingly within arm's reach. And yet, though I could hear them, they still refused to reveal themselves to me. And I held my head perfectly still, and opened my eyes wide, and searched for them, quietly shifting my eyes from left to right and back again. And then, as suddenly as they appeared, they silenced themselves again, and the chatter of their voices gave way to the mundane sounds of the court proceedings.

And I narrowed my eyes and gazed toward the witness stand, and as I did, I saw Officer Johnson rise from his seat and leave the courtroom. Then I saw the attorneys for the prosecution gather around the table, their eyes cast longingly upon a yellow pad. I assumed they were trying to decide which witness to call next. As they conferred among themselves, I looked about again, ever aware that those on the other side of the rail were looking at me. I longed for this to be over, one way or the other, for try as I may, I could not bring myself to care.

Then suddenly I saw one of the attorneys raise his head and look about the room before calling my aunt to the stand; I averted my eyes as she pushed through the swinging doors and slowly made her way past me. As she did, she hesitated and gently placed her hand upon my shoulder. Yet, I refused to look at her. I was determined to blot out her image and quiet her voice, and place distance between myself and the pain I was convinced her words were about to cause.

"Do you know the defendant?" I heard the prosecutor's first question, and I felt my aunt's eyes on my face but I refused to look.

"Yes, sir," she said. "He's my nephew." Then I heard her voice break and I closed my eyes and prayed to God, asking him to help her through this.

"Have you ever had occasion to see the defendant strike his wife?" the prosecutor asked, and instantly there was a deafening silence, which answered the question long before she could. I prayed to God again, asking him to strengthen her. I bowed my head. I could feel her eyes on me.

"Yes, sir," she said, her voice barely above a whisper.

The prosecutor paused again—I knew he had done so simply for effect. Yes, I had hit my wife once, so it only stood to reason that I would hit her again. At least that's what he wanted them to think.

"Was he arrested?" the prosecutor asked.

Then suddenly the passage of time loomed before me as stark and as bright as the stars in the sky above, and I was there again, in the stale, parched air, my child lying in a house of intoxicated strangers, and my wife standing angrily before me, filling the doorway, denying me access.

"Yes, sir," Daphne said, and I felt the pain in her voice, a pain that bespoke the agony of one whose task it had become to utter the words that would seal the fate of the one whom she loved.

"Did the case go to trial?" he asked.

"No, sir," she said, and I sensed that she was searching for a way to steer clear of the course down which she unwittingly was being led.

"How was it resolved?"

"He pled guilty," she said, and the prosecutor paused to let the full sound of her words reverberate throughout the court.

"Was he sentenced to prison?"

"No, sir," she said. "He was given probation."

"What were the terms of his probation?"

"He was given community service," she said, then paused, not wanting to say more."

"And," the prosecutor said, pressing her.

"He was ordered to seek marriage counseling."

"And," the prosecutor said, then waited.

"He was ordered to attended anger management classes."

"Anger management?" The prosecutor repeated the words.

"Yes, sir." she said.

"So the court determines that he had an anger management problem?"

"I don't know, sir," she said. "You would have to ask the court."

"Fair enough," he said.

I glanced up. My aunt was looking at me. I quickly averted my eyes and patiently waited for all this to be over.

"Did you ever hear Mr. Jackson say that he killed his wife?"

My aunt hesitated, and I knew she was looking for a way out. But what way did she have? I had said it. She had heard me say it, and they all knew it. Otherwise, why would they ask? In my mind, I could hear her saying, *No, sir . . . Never . . .* But how could she, when we all knew that wasn't true.

She remained silent, pondering the question. The prosecutor spoke again: "Mrs. Gipson," he said. "May I remind you that you are under oath."

Yes, a cop had been present when I had spoken about Juanita. And yes, I had said what they claimed I said. But they were twisting my words. They were taking them out of context. That's what she would tell them. That's how she would answer.

"He didn't mean it like that," she said.

The prosecutor frowned angrily.

I didn't ask you what he meant," he snapped. "I asked if you ever heard the defendant say he killed his wife."

There was silence.

"Your Honor," he said after a moment or two, "please instruct the witness to answer the question."

"Mrs. Gipson," he said, "answer the question or I will hold you in contempt of court."

Suddenly, I heard my aunt sigh.

"Yes, sir," she said. "I did."

Again, a murmur rose from the court. The judge tapped his gavel and the room became quiet again. The prosecutor whirled dramatically and faced the judge.

"No further questions," he said. Then he returned to the prosecution's table and took a seat. Next to me, Mr. Lawson rose and approached the witness stand. My aunt looked at him. Her eyes were sullen.

"Where were you when Mr. Jackson made that statement?"

"In the visitation room."

"At the jail?"

"Yes, sir."

"Did he explain to you what he meant?"

"Yes, sir."

"What did he say?"

"He said that he didn't kill them but he was responsible for their deaths."

"Did he explain what he meant by that?"

"Yes, sir," she said.

"What did he tell you?"

"He said that he should have been home. He said that if he had, then none of this would have happened."

"So, in actuality, he said he didn't kill them, didn't he?"

"Yes, sir," she said.

"Thank you," he said. Then he turned to the judge. "Nothing further, Your Honor."

He returned to the table and took his seat. The prosecutor rose and addressed my aunt again.

"Where was the defendant on the night of the murder?" he asked.

"I don't know."

"You don't know?" he said. "Didn't he tell you?"

She hesitated again.

"Please answer the question," he said forcefully.

"He said he went to the hotel in Cedar Lake."

"Did he?"

My aunt hesitated again.

"Please answer the question," the prosecutor said.

"As far as I know," she said.

"Doesn't his cell phone record show that he was actually in Natchez, Mississippi, and not Cedar Lake?"

"That's what I hear," she said.

"So he lied."

"Yes, sir," she said. "I guess so."

"Nothing further," he said.

I watched my aunt leave the courtroom and I could tell she was bothered by the testimony she was forced to give, and I could tell that she was afraid for me. I nodded to her and smiled faintly as she passed. My mind was squarely on her when I heard the prosecution call his next witness.

"The prosecution calls Mrs. Felicia Fontenot."

At that moment, I would rather have been anywhere than here. There was a pen and a yellow legal pad on the table before me. I lifted the pen and began doodling on the pad. Felicia entered the courtroom and took a seat on the witness stand. I could hear the prosecutor approaching her, but I did not look; instead, I kept my eyes averted.

"State your name for the record," he said.

"Felicia Fontenot," she said, and when she did, I heard the demons again. They were laughing—no, they were taunting me.

"Ms. Fontenot, do you know the defendant?"

"I do," she said.

I knew she was looking at me. I could feel her eyes on me. But I kept my eyes averted. I kept doodling on the pad.

"A few days ago the defendant hired an attorney," he said. "A very good attorney at that. Do you know who paid for it?"

"Yes, sir."

"Who?"

"I did," she said, and I felt myself bear down hard on the pencil.

I did not know that. I wanted to look but my eyes would not stray. I felt my face flush warm. I glanced at the glass of water on the table before me. I wanted a drink. Yes, that would calm me. In my mind, I could see myself reaching for the glass and raising it to my lips. I commanded my hand to do so, but it refused to move. I was frozen. I was paralyzed.

"He also hired a private investigator, didn't he?"

"Yes, sir," she said.

"Who paid for it?"

"I did."

"Did the defendant attempt suicide a few days ago?"

"Yes, sir."

"How?"

"He shot himself in the head."

"Did he lose consciousness?"

"Yes, sir."

"Who revived him?"

"I did."

"Are you the defendant's guardian angel?"

"No," I said. "I'm his friend."

"Friend," he said. "Or lover?"

Suddenly, my attorney leaped to his feet.

"Objection," he yelled.

"Sustained," the judge retorted. A murmur swept the court. Then the judge pounded his gavel and the court became quiet again. Only now, I could feel their eyes on me but I did not care. I squeezed the pencil tighter and bore down hard on the long sheet of yellow paper lying before me.

"When was the last time you spoke to him prior to the murder?"

"I don't know exactly."

"Approximately."

"Twenty-two years ago," she said.

I shifted my feet a little, but I still did not look up. I kept my eyes squarely on the paper. I had drawn a crude stick man, and I had scribbled a few unrelated words, but now I was simply moving the pencil back and forth with no purpose or intent in mind except to keep my eyes from straying toward the stand.

"When was the last time you had seen him?"

"Twenty-two years ago."

"What was the nature of your relationship twenty-two years ago?"

"We were dating."

"Were you intimate?"

Mr. Lawson rose again and voiced his objection. The judge overruled him and Felicia answered the question.

"Yes, sir," she said calmly.

"So the two of you were having sex?"

"Yes, sir," she said.

"Was he the first boy you ever had sex with?"

Mr. Lawson objected again. The judge overruled him.

"Yes, sir," she said. "He was the first."

"Did he break up with you or did you break up with him?"

"He broke up with me."

"Why?"

She was silent for a moment. Then she answered him.

"He met someone else."

"Who did he meet?"

She paused again. "Juanita Miller," she said.

The sound of my wife's name jolted me. I closed my eyes for a moment and took a deep breath. I heard the demons laugh again. I wanted to rise from my seat and strike out at them, make them leave, but I remained seated, only now my leg was trembling.

"His future wife?" the prosecutor asked.

"Yes, sir," she said.

"How did you take it?"

"Take what, sir?"

"Seeing the two of them together."

"Not too well."

She hesitated, and I felt that she was looking at me. And I felt as if she wanted to cry but I was not certain. My head was still down. I refused to look at her. I just couldn't.

"Do you still love him?"

She hesitated.

"Please answer the question."

"Yes, sir," she said. "I do."

A murmur swept the courtroom. The judge pounded his gavel. I knew she was looking at me, but I still refused to look.

"Prior to her murder, a female called Mrs. Jackson and told her that her husband was running around with another woman. Were you the person who called?"

"No, sir, I was not."

"You didn't like Mrs. Jackson, did you?"

"I didn't know her."

"You knew she took your man, correct?"

"That was a long time ago."

"But you never got over it, did you?"

"No, sir," she said.

"You still love him, don't you?"

"Yes, sir," she said. "I do."

Behind me, I heard several people gasp. Then I heard the prosecutor's voice again.

"Nothing further," he said.

"Your witness," the judge told Mr. Lawson.

"I have no questions for this witness at this time," Mr. Lawson said. Then I heard the judge's voice again.

"You may be excused," he said.

I heard Felicia rise and walk from the courtroom. And as she did, my head was down and my eyes were averted. I was doodling.

CHAPTER 41

After I testified, I went outside. There was a little gazebo situated just off the courthouse lawn. I was sitting in the gazebo watching the passing traffic, pondering what had just transpired inside the courtroom. Yes, I still loved Luther and I did not care who knew. And I was thinking about that when detective Gray approached me.

"It looks bleak," I said, "doesn't it?"

"Bleaker by the minute," he said.

"I still say he didn't kill his family."

"If he didn't," he said, "I don't know who did."

"Someone knows," I said. "I'm convinced of that."

He climbed onto the gazebo and took a seat on the bench across from me. I was facing Main Street and he was facing the courthouse. I saw him looking at the building but I knew he wasn't seeing it. He was thinking about what I had just said.

"Well, we just have to flush them out," he said.

"And how do you propose we do that?"

"Money," he said.

I squinted. I was not exactly sure what he meant.

"A reward," he said. "We need to offer a reward."

"Do you think that will work?"

"If is doesn't," he said, "nothing will."

I paused, thinking.

"How much money?" I asked.

"It has to be sizable."

"How sizable?"

He paused again, and I knew he was turning the numbers over in his head. "Sizable enough to make somebody rat out a loved one," he said. "Or a friend."

"And how much is that?"

"How much can you afford?"

"You just tell me what we need," I said, "and I will get it."

"Twenty-five thousand," he said.

I was quiet.

"Can you afford it?"

"I can afford it," I said.

"Are you sure about this?"

"I'm sure."

"What if he's guilty?" he asked.

"Then at least I will know."

And that evening, I set aside the money, and together we contacted the media, and we placed ads in the papers, and gave interviews to the regional radio and television stations, and we printed flyers, and I saw Joshua again, and I asked him to bring some of his friends by my house. I hired them to canvass the streets and pass out flyers, and spreading the word that I would pay thirty thousand dollars to anyone providing information that led to the capture and conviction of the person or persons responsible for the murder of Juanita and Darnell Jackson.

CHAPTER 42

At five minutes after two, Mrs. Olivia Washington took the stand. She looked at me only once, then she stared straight ahead, answering each question as if she had already heard it before, and while she was speaking, I looked over my shoulder, trying to see Felicia. But neither Felicia nor my aunt was present in the courtroom, and I realized that since they were now witnesses, they would not be allowed to sit in the jury room during the remainder of the proceedings. And I felt grateful to Felicia for all that she had done but I also felt bad for all that I knew she was going through.

I watched Miss Olivia climb onto the witness stand, and I listened to her tell how she had worked at the high school for nearly thirty years, and how she had been baptized as a child of twelve, and how she had stayed faithful to God and worked diligently in the church, and how she had never had a problem with anyone in the community, including me. And then, I watched the prosecutor furrow his brow and clench his fist, and I saw him pause and purse his lips, and I saw him turn from her and look at me. Then I heard him ask the question for which this entire show had been enacted.

"Do you know who killed Juanita Jackson?"

And there was a hush over the room. Time seemed to slow, and the space between his question and her answer seemed vast.

"Yes, sir," she said.

"Who?" he asked.

"Luther Jackson," she spoke my name.

The courtroom erupted. The judge pounded the gavel. And the entire time, Miss Olivia sat tall in her chair with her hands folded across her lap, and yes, she was looking at me. The entire time, she was looking at me.

"Do you know who killed Darnell Jackson?"

"Yes, sir," she said.

"Who?" the prosecutor asked.

"Luther Jackson."

The courtroom erupted again. The judge pounded the gavel again. And the whole time, Miss Olivia sat tall in her chair with her hands folded across her lap, staring at me.

"Do you see the man you referred to as Luther Jackson any-where in the courtroom?" the prosecutor asked.

"Yes, sir," she said, and she was still staring at me.

"Could you point him out?"

"Yes, sir," she said.

And I saw her slowly raise her hand and point at me, and when she did, she did not blink, nor did her hand quiver. No, her hand was steady, and her voice was calm, and she stared directly at me.

"Why?" I heard someone shout behind me. I did not turn, nor did I look. I did not have to. It was Juanita's mother. Suddenly, she screamed again, and through the shouts of the others, I heard her voice clearly: "Why did you have to kill her? Why?"

And then, I heard the judge pound the gavel again. And I heard the sound of shuffled feet on the floor behind me. And I heard heavy breathing, and I knew the bailiff was struggling to remove Mrs. Miller from the courtroom. And I heard her scream *Why* again, and I heard the door leading into the courtroom open, and I heard her yell again. "I hope you rot in hell." And then I heard the laughter again. No, not from within the courtroom, but from the demons, looking on from some distant plane—cloaked in secrecy, visible to no one but themselves, audible to no one but me.

I wanted to leap from my seat and challenge all that had been said, but I remained still and calm, and I continued to look at Miss Olivia as she continued to look at me. I heard someone behind me sobbing heavily. It was not the delicate sound of a woman's voice; instead, it was the heavy sound of a tormented man, and without looking, I knew the voice. I knew it well—it was Juanita's father.

"Are you certain?" the prosecutor asked.

"I'm certain," she said, and her voice did not quake nor did it quiver.

"What did you hear that night?"

"I heard them arguing," she said. "He was yelling and screaming at the top of his voice."

"About what?"

"I don't know," she said. "But I heard her tell him to go away. And I heard her tell him to never come back. And I heard her tell him to go find the woman he was running around with. And I heard her tell him to go live with her. And I heard her tell him that she did not want him no more."

"And what did he say?"

"He said he wasn't going anywhere."

"And what did she say?"

"She said that she was leaving and he told her she wasn't. I heard her say, try and stop me. That's when they started fighting. I guess she threw something at him, because I heard something break. It sounded like glass. And then I heard him say, if you hit me with that, I'll kill you."

"He said that?"

"Yes, sir."

"Then what happened?"

"I guess she threw something else, because I heard a loud crash. And then it sounded like all hell broke loose over there. They started yelling and screaming, and I heard things breaking. And I heard him call her an ugly name. And then I heard her scream at the top of her lungs. And then it was quiet. Real quiet."

"About what time was that?"

"A little after ten."

"Then what happened?"

"About fifteen minutes later, I saw him leave the house."

"The defendant?"

"Yes, sir."

"Was he running?"

"No, sir. But he was walking fast."

"Did you see where he went?"

"Yes, sir."

"Where did he go?"

"He got in his car and drove off."

"Was he alone?'

"Yes, sir."

"Was he carrying anything?"

"Yes sir?"

"What was he carrying?"

"A gasoline can."

"Nothing further," he said.

I leaned over and whispered into my attorney's ear. "None of it's true," I said. "I swear." I knew my words meant very little to him, and I was angry with myself for having uttered them. I lifted the pencil and began doodling again. This hearing had nothing to do with me. This was simply a game that I had very little interest in playing.

Mr. Lawson rose and approached the stand but I didn't look at Olivia, I continued to doodle.

"You saw Mr. Johnson carrying a gasoline can?" he said, his voice forceful, aggressive.

"Yes, sir," she said. "I did."

"That's not what you said in your original statement."

"It's what I'm saying now," she retorted.

"So, you're changing your testimony?" he pressed her.

No, sir," she said. "I'm just telling you what I saw."

"What you saw, and what you heard, seems to have changed since you were deposed, hasn't it?"

"No, sir," she said. "It hasn't. I heard Luther Jackson say, I'm going to kill you. And I saw him run from his house. And he was carrying a gas can."

"You heard him say, I'm going to kill you?"

"Yes, sir."

"Did you tell that to the police on the night in question?" he said, then waiting for her response. But she didn't answer.

"Well, did you?" he asked.

"No, sir," she said.

"Why not?"

"I was too shaken."

"Did you include that in your original statement?"

"No, sir."

"Why not?"

"I didn't want to believe it."

"You didn't want to believe it?"

"No, sir," she said. "And I was scared."

"Scared of what?"

"Luther Jackson," she said. "He lives next door. I was afraid he would kill me like he killed them."

"Did you see him kill his wife and child?"

No," she said. "But I heard him say, I'll kill you. Then I heard her scream. And then I didn't hear her say anything else."

"What time was that?"

"A little after ten."

"Did you call the police?"

"No, sir," she said.

"Why not?"

"I don't know."

"You witnessed a murder and you did not call the police?"

"No, sir."

"Did you call anyone?"

"No sir."

"What did you do?"

"I don't remember."

"Did you go to bed?"

"I think so."

"You were too afraid to call the police but you were not too afraid to go to sleep."

"No, sir," she said. "I guess not."

"Do you live alone?"

"Yes, sir."

"Weren't you afraid to be in the house alone with a murderer on the loose?"

"Yes, sir."

"So why didn't you call someone?"

"I don't know."

"Don't you think you should have warned your neighbors?"

"I don't know."

"Don't you think you should have gotten help for Mrs. Jackson and her child?"

"I don't know," she said.

"You don't know?" he said. "Didn't you just testify to your strong affinity for the church?"

"Yes, sir."

"Well," he said, "a woman and her child were hurt. And you witnessed it. Don't you think calling an ambulance or the police would have been the Christian thing to do?"

"They fought all the time," she said. "I didn't think this was any different. I figured he might have roughed her up some. But I didn't know that he had killed her."

"But you just testified that you saw him kill her."

"I didn't know she was dead at the time," she said.

"You didn't know because you didn't see it," he said. "Did you?"

"I told you what I saw," she said.

"What time do you normally go to bed?"

"Nine-thirty," she said. "Maybe ten."

"What time did you go to bed that night?"

"Ten-thirty," she said. "Maybe eleven."

"So you witnessed a murder at a little after ten and you went to bed a few minutes later."

"Yes, sir."

"Mrs. Washington, do you expect this court to believe that?"

"I don't care what you believe."

"Do you care about the truth?"

"Yes sir," she said. "I do."

"Then why don't you try telling it?"

"Objection, Your Honor."

"Sustained."

"Nothing further," he said, and as he walked back to the table, I looked at Miss Olivia, and I wondered why she was lying.

CHAPTER 43

My cell phone rang. On the other end was the voice of a boy. He uttered four simple words: *"Look for a watch."*

My first inclination was to hang up. Since the reward had been posted, I had been inundated with calls. Most of them were ridiculous, one or two seem credible, but none amounted to much more than conjecture. So, when this one came in, I immediately thought that like the others, this was simply another person casting out a line in hopes of reeling in what the townfolks were calling "the Luther L. Jackson sweepstakes."

"Excuse me," I said, and then waited.

"Look for a watch," he said again.

"What kind of watch?"

"A little kid's watch."

I paused again, hoping that he would say more, but when he did not, I questioned him further.

"Where?" I asked.

"On Elm Street."

"Where on Elm?"

"That's all I can say," he said.

"Is this some kind of joke?" I asked. "Because if it is, I don't think it's very funny."

"This is no joke," he said.

"Well, I don't understand."

"I'm sorry," he said. "But when you find the watch, you will understand."

"Are you serious?"

"Yes, ma'am," he said.

"But what does this have to do with the murders?"

"That's all I can say," he said. Then he hung up.

I called the detective and he agreed that it made no sense. What kind of watch? How would we know it when we found it? Where on Elm Street were we supposed to look? And, what did it have to do with this case?

"No," he said. "This doesn't sound like anything to me. Go to bed and let's go at it again tomorrow."

"Do you think he should plead?" I asked.

"I'm not his lawyer," he said. "But if I were, I would advise him to take the deal before the prosecutor withdraws his offer. There is too much evidence against him. If he goes to trial, I believe he will be convicted."

"But if he pleads guilty," I said, "he will spend the rest of his life in prison."

"And if he doesn't," the detective said, "chances are he will be executed."

I stretched out across the bed but I could not sleep. How does one sleep when the dawning of tomorrow promises so much pain? This just could not be happening. I was a smart woman. And he was a smart man. There had to be something that I could do to right the wrong that I saw looming on the horizon. Suddenly, in the midst of that thought, the phone rang again. I answered it. It was Detective Gray.

"What if it wasn't about her?" he asked.

"Excuse me?"

"What if it was about the kid?"

"I don't understand."

"The caller said to look for a kid's watch, correct?"

"That's right."

"Did Darnell Jackson own a watch?"

"I don't know."

"When we stated that nothing was missing from the house, we only examined her belongings," he said. "We did not examine the kid's."

"Why would someone steal a kid's watch?" I asked. "And why would they kill him for it? That doesn't make any sense."

"I don't know," he said. "But what if the killer's beef was with the kid and not with her?"

"What kind of beef could someone possibly have with a child that small? It just doesn't make sense," I said again.

"There are all kinds of sick people in this world," he said. "And what doesn't make sense to us makes perfect sense to them."

"I don't know."

"Meet me at the jail in the morning," he said. "We need to talk to Mr. Jackson. In the meantime, I'm going to give Peter a call."

"Okay," I said, and I hung up the phone and went to bed but I could not sleep. So, I rose, and paced the floor. And I prayed for morning to hurry up and come. And I vowed that in the morning, I would go to Elm Street, and I would knock on doors, and I would look for a watch. And when I found it, I hoped that this would all be over.

CHAPTER 44

Mr. Gray asked me if Darnell owned a watch. I thought the question strange but I told him that he did, and I told him that it was a sports watch, one that he had received for his tenth birthday, and he asked me what it looked like, and I told him that it was silver and black and that the face bore the emblem of his favorite football team, the Oakland Raiders, and he thanked me and left, and Felicia went with him, and in the next instant, I was transported to a courtroom where I sat behind the table, confused, as my lawyer requested a recess, which the judge granted, and I was taken to the basement and placed in the holding cell, and as the door clanged shut, I was wondering what was going on and why no one was telling me anything.

Unlike at the jail, in the courthouse holding area there was a window in the cell. For nearly half an hour, I stood in the window, with my back to the seven or eight other guys in the cell with me. Outside, I could see several people milling about the courthouse square and I wondered if I would ever again exist in the world beyond these bars. Oh, how cruel was my fate? And how long would I be forced to live in the world of those deemed unfit for society when my only crime had been an error in judgment that had already taken from me more than the state of Louisiana ever could?

At 1:15, the bailiff returned and escorted me back to the courtroom, and I was sitting next to my lawyer, staring at the large flag behind the judge when the bailiff passed the note to my attorney. I watched him read it, then instantly rise to his feet.

"Permission to approach the bench," he said.

And there was giddiness in his voice, and a spring in his step, and I wondered what was going on. I leaned forward, watching the lawyers banter back and forth before the judge, and I saw the judge scratch his head and take the note from my lawyer, and the lawyers went back to their respective tables, and then Mr. Lawson rose and said:

"The defense calls Joshua Edwards to the stand."

And I watched a young boy of fifteen sheepishly make his way into the courtroom. His head was held low, and his body was stiff, and his hands were clasped nervously before his crotch. He climbed the stairs and took a seat. He glanced at me knowingly, then quickly lowered his eyes.

"Raise your right hand."

He raised his hand but kept his eyes averted.

"Do you swear to tell the truth, the whole truth, and nothing but the truth, so help you God?"

"Yes, sir," he said, his voice cracking slightly. "I do."

"State your name for the record."

"Joshua Edwards."

And then I recognized him. That was Philip Edwards's boy. I had seen him and his papa at the machine shop collecting the empty soda cans from the trash bins after work.

"Good afternoon, Joshua," he said.

"Afternoon," he replied.

I leaned forward, looking at him. What was this all about? Why hadn't anybody told me anything?

"Joshua, how old are you?" Mr. Lawson asked. I saw the boy look up briefly. He hesitated, then answered.

"Fifteen," he said.

"Where do you live?"

"In Brownsville," he said, this time keeping his eyes averted. I glanced at the judge—he had been leaning back in his seat, but now he was sitting upright, looking directly at the boy.

"Where in Brownsville?" he asked.

"Elm Street," the boy said.

"Do you know the defendant?" Mr. Lawson asked, and I saw the boy look at me, then quickly look away.

"Yes, sir," he said.

"Who is he?"

"Mr. Jackson."

"How do you know Mr. Jackson?"

"We live in the same neighborhood," he said.

"On the same street?"

"No, sir. He lives on Turner Drive."

"Did you know Mr. Jackson's son?"

"Yes, sir."

"Did you know his wife?"

"Yes, sir. She teaches at my school. At least she used to before she died. I mean, before she got killed."

"Do you know why Mr. Jackson is here?"

"Yes, sir."

"Why?"

"They say he killed his family."

"Did he?"

Suddenly, the boy became quiet. I looked at him and frowned. What was this all about?

"No, sir," he said.

A murmur swept the courtroom. The judge pounded the gavel, yelling, "Order . . . Order . . . Order in the court."

"Who killed them?"

"Curtis the kook."

Again, the courtroom erupted and again the judge pounded the gavel. Only this time the district attorney leaped to his feet. "What is this, Peter?" he screamed. "What are you trying to pull here?"

"Order . . . Order . . Order in the court."

"Who?" Mr. Lawson pressed on.

"Curtis Jones."

I fell back against the chair. I felt my chest rising and falling. I heard the demons again, calling to me from far away. Murderer . . . Murderer," they screamed. Inside, I felt myself raging against the name that belonged to the person who had taken all from me.

"What did you call him?" I heard Mr. Lawson say.

"Curtis the kook," he said.

"Why?"

"I guess because of the way he acts."

"And how does he act?"

"Crazy," he said.

The district attorney stood again and stared at the judge. "Objection, Your Honor," he yelled. "Objection."

"Overruled," I head the judge say.

Again, I felt my heart pounding. I did not understand. None of this made sense. Curtis was just a kid. What was going on? Why was this happening? I willed my mind steady. I forced myself to listen.

"Please tell us what happened," Mr. Lawson continued.

"She was frying chicken," he said.

"Who was frying chicken?"

"Mrs. Jackson."

"How do you know that?"

"We could smell it."

"What do you mean by *we*?"

"Baby Boy, Juwan, Pee Wee, Curtis, and me."

"Where were you all?"

"We were standing in the street in front of her house."

I sighed and closed my eyes. I could see the long, narrow street running past my house, and I could see my house sitting back off the street. And I could see the large oak tree sitting out front, casting long shadows in the summertime and creating peaceful solitude in the drabness of the winter. And I could see Juanita, standing in the kitchen before a hot stove, and I could smell the fresh scent of frying chicken filling the house with the comforting aroma of home and I looked at him sitting before me, telling the tale of how this all came to pass, and I could hear the weary voice of my dejected soul screaming *Why*.

"He likes fried chicken," I heard Joshua say, and his words drifted to me as if from some imaginary place far, far away. No, this was not real. It was a dream from which I would awaken any minute now.

"He likes it?" Mr. Lawson said.

"No, sir," he said. "He *loves* fried chicken."

"Then what happened?"

"Curtis knocked on the door."

"Why?"

"I guess he was going to ask Mrs. Jackson to give him a piece of that chicken."

"Did he?"

"Yes, sir,"

"Then what happened?"

"She told him to leave with his crazy self. And not to come around there anymore."

"And what did he do?"

"He got mad."

"Did he leave?"

"Yes, sir."

"Where did he go?"

"He came back to the street where we were."

"What happened next?"

"We started teasing him."

"You and the boys?"

"Yes, sir."

"Then what happened?"

"He acted like he was going to cry, so we stopped."

"What happened next?"

"We messed around for a few hours, then we went back to Juwan's house."

"What did you do over there?"

"Played dominoes. Drank some beer. And got high."

"Got high on what?"

"Weed."

"Marijuana?"

"Yes, sir."

"Did Curtis drink and get high, too?"

"Yes, sir."

"Then what happened?"

"Baby Boy started messing with him again."

"What do you mean?"

"Teasing him about what had happened. And telling him that he ought to go back over there and take a piece of that chicken."

"Then what happened?"

"Pee Wee told him just because he was slow didn't mean he had to let people talk to him like that."

"What did he say?"

"Nothing at first. But Baby Boy kept egging him on and kept giving him stuff to drink."

"Then what happened?"

"Curtis started getting mad again. And then we saw Mr. Jackson leave in his truck."

"About what time was that?"

"Almost ten o'clock."

"How do you know?"

"We have a 10:30 curfew," he said. "So, we were watching the time."

"Then what happened?"

"Baby Boy told Curtis to go pee on Mrs. Jackson's front porch," he said, and I saw Mr. Lawson tilt his head and look at him strangely.

"Pee!" he said.

"Yes, sir," the boy said, and his voice trailed away and Mr. Lawson paused, and the boy lowered his head, embarrassed.

"Did he?" Mr. Lawson asked.

"Yes, sir," the boy said, his voice barely above a whisper.

Mr. Lawson paused again, and I stared at the boy. I willed him to look at me, but he refused; his eyes remained averted, his head remained down. I wanted to rise from my seat and shout, "Look at me!" But I remained seated with my hands folded tightly across my lap. My legs were shaking, and I could feel myself gently rocking back and forth.

"Where were you boys?"

"Standing in the street."

I closed my eyes again. In my mind, I could see them lolling in the street before my house. Baby Boy, Juwan, Pee Wee, Curtis, and him. Why? I heard the voice scream inside me. Why did this have to happen?

"Then what happened?"

"I guess Mrs. Jackson saw him, because she opened the door and told him to leave before she called the police."

You should have been home, I heard the voice inside me say. And I cupped my hands over my ears and bowed my head over the table. I knew that the voice had spoken the truth—I should have been home, protecting my family from the evil lurking beyond my front door.

"What did you all do?"

"We ran."

"Where did you go?"

"Back to Juwan's house."

"Then what happened?"

"About ten minutes later we saw Curtis walking down the street, eating a piece of chicken."

"And what time was that?"

"A little after ten," he said.

"Did you talk to him?"

"Yes, sir."

"What did he say?"

"Just that he loved fried chicken."

"Then what happened?"

"He showed us the watch."

"Whose watch was it?"

"Darnell Jackson's."

I shook my head and squeezed my ears harder. Oh, this was

too much. "Stand and leave," I heard the voice say. And I wanted to leap from my chair, and run from the room. But where would I go? What would I do? I could see my son, clutching his watch, struggling against the manchild who would take it from him.

"How did he get it?"

"He said he took it."

Their words came to me now, as if from a faraway place. Dim, unwelcome, tormenting.

"What happened to Darnell?"

"Curtis killed him."

I laid my head on the table and cried. In the distance I heard my son calling to me. *Help me, Daddy . . . Please help me.*

"How did he kill him?"

"He beat him to death with one of Mr. Jackson's golf clubs."

"He told you that?"

"Yes, sir."

"Why did he kill?"

"Because Darnell wouldn't turn the watch a-loose."

"What happened to Mrs. Jackson?"

"He killed her, too."

I was there again, and their slain bodies were lying upon the floor and I was standing over them, and my body was taut, and my eyes were wet, and my mind refused to grasp what reality told me was real.

"How?" Mr. Lawson continued to press.

"They were in the kitchen. I don't think he was trying to kill her. He was trying to get a piece of chicken. She tried to stop him and he slung her into the table. I guess she hit her head on something. I don't know."

"Who burned the bodies?"

"He did."

I couldn't stop crying. Beyond my tears, I could smell the strong, pungent odor of their burning flesh, and I could see the charred remains of their mangled bodies, and it was all too real again. And I longed for it to be over—the questions, the hearing, the nightmare.

"Why?"

"I guess because that's what he does at work."

"I don't understand."

"We all work for Mr. Gattis."

"Who is Mr. Gattis?"

"A pig farmer."

"I still don't understand."

"When one of his hogs die we burn the body to keep the disease from spreading. Usually we cover the hog with wood and douse the wood with gasoline or diesel to get the fire started."

"Oh," he said. "I see."

"I guess Curtis thought that's what you do to people when they die."

"Did he tell you that they were dead?"

"Yes, sir. He said he had killed them."

"Did you believe him?"

"Yes, sir."

"Why?"

"Because he had blood on his clothes and he smelled like gasoline."

"What happened to the gasoline can?"

"Curtis had left it in the yard. Pee Wee went down there and got it, then he threw it away. He was scared it might have Curtis's fingerprints on it."

"Where did he throw it?"

"In the catfish pond on the other side of town."

"Why didn't you tell anybody about this?"

"I was scared," he said. "We all were."

"Why are you telling it now?"

"Because the detective found out about it."

"Mr. Gray?"

"Yes, sir."

He paused and shook his head.

"What were you boys thinking?"

"I don't know, sir."

"Didn't you boys know that Curtis was on medication?"

"No, sir."

"But you did know that he was mentally challenged?"

"Yes, sir."

"And you knew that he was intoxicated, or at least under the influence of alcohol and marijuana, didn't you?"

"Yes, sir."

"So what did you boys think was going to happen?"

"We didn't know."

"You didn't know?"

"No sir," he said. "We were just teasing him. That's all. Nobody knew that something like this would happen."

"Something like what?"

"That he would kill them."

He said that, the judge pounded the gavel, and just like that, it was all over.

CHAPTER 45

I gazed into his eyes, and there were in me no thoughts of the past, or of the future, only joy that he and I were together at this time and at this place, and that his ordeal was over, and from this moment on, he and I were free to explore the love that we shared long ago. I was giddy inside at the prospect of feeling his soft, gentle hands moving slowly and tenderly over my excited body. And I yearned inside for him. And I was not concerned with the neighbors, or his family, or my family.

No, I was not concerned. I simply wanted to draw him into me, and love him as he deserved to be loved. I closed my eyes and snuggled closer. His arms were about me, and my legs were entwined with his, and I could feel the warmth of his breath on the nape of my neck. And my body tingled for him. "I love you," I whispered. I had not intended to say it, at least not at that precise moment. But it is what I felt. It is what I have always felt.

I moved closer to him. And I slowly unbuttoned his shirt, and I gently touched his nipple with the tip of my finger. And I didn't care that I was in her house, or that I was stretched out on her bed, but I did care that he seemed a little distant and a little stiff. Though my body yearned for him, I told myself that I could be patient. No, I *would* be patient. If now was not the moment, I would wait, and I would give myself to him on another day or at another time, when his body spoke to him then as my body was speaking to me now. And I told myself that, and mentally I meant it, but my body ached for him, and though I knew I must be respectful of him and his situation, I gave in to my body and I snuggled a little closer, and I gently pressed my breast against his naked flesh, and I waited to see if his body would react to me. And I spoke to him without speaking, asking him to make love to me. And I waited, hoping to hear his answer.

Then I felt his hands gently pulling me on top of him. And suddenly, I was sixteen again, and it was my prom night, and he and I had parked by the lake. The stars were bright, the gentle breeze was cool, and we were lying on a blanket, and we were naked, and he was making love to me, outside, under the stars, in the quiet, peaceful solitude of the moonlit lake.

And suddenly, my heart was in my throat, and I leaned forward and laid my head upon his chest, and I felt his hand in the small of my back, and I closed my eyes, feeling the sensation that his simple touch has caused in me, and I was reveling in his touch, and longing for more, when I heard the sirens again. And suddenly, I felt his hands fall from me, and I felt his body shift and then ease away until he was separated from me, and I turned my head toward the window, and I cursed the sirens for trying to keep us apart. And I looked at him, and I wanted to speak aloud to him. I wanted to ask him not to go, but words would not come. So I curled next to him again, and I tried to whisper to him without speaking. But the sirens had him. He rose from the bed, and I followed him out onto the porch, and we looked toward Miss Olivia's house.

Hot flames leaped from the windows. Black clouds of suffocating smoke ascended high into the sky. In the streets, a woman screamed. Her wail made me turn and look.

"She's still in there," she shouted, pointing toward the house.

"Help her!" came the frantic pleas of another.

I saw Luther leap to the ground and dash toward the house, and when he was upon her porch, I saw him jiggle the doorknob. And in that instant, my heart began to pound, and I raced toward the burning building, and I stretched forth my hands and I called to him, but he did not answer.

And I looked beyond him, seeing the red and yellow flames leaping outward and rising higher and higher into the dry evening air. Then I looked at him again and I saw him step back, then kick the door hard. The door flew open. And instantly, the flames roared higher. I yelled to him, but he did not answer. I stepped toward the porch but the hot flames forced me back. I saw him cover his face with his arms, and I saw him duck his head against the heat. Then I saw him dip his shoulder and disappear inside the flaming inferno. Behind me I heard someone scream.

And I sank to the ground—I cried for him, and I prayed for him, and I heard the sirens again. And I heard people moving about. But I refused to look. Instead, I continued to pray. Then I heard a loud noise. And I heard someone say the roof had caved in, and I heard a woman scream again, and suddenly, I was in a deep, dark, void, seeing nothing but hearing everything.

The fire truck arrived, and more people gathered, and I could hear the confused chatter of those who would make sense of this thing. Then the chief arrived, and so did A. J., and it all seemed so surreal to me. There was the gush of water, and the loud crackling of the flames, and through it all I continued to pray. And then Luther emerged, and he was carrying Miss Olivia in his arms, and his back was bent from the heavy weight of her.

And he staggered from the house and he laid her body gently upon the grass. Then he fell to the ground. His feet were charred, his clothes smoldering. I heard him cough, then gasp for breath. And I placed my arms around him and I cradled his head upon my lap; and his flesh was hot, and his hair was singed, and I called to him, and when he did not answer, I bent low to blow air into his smoke-filled lungs, and just as I did, his eyes opened and he gazed wearily into my eyes. I saw him frown. And my face was only inches from his face.

"Juanita," I heard him whisper. And my eyes clouded, and then I knew: she was to him, as he was to me.

"Go to her," I said.

I saw him look toward the heavens, and upon his face was a smile. Then I saw him close his eyes. And I felt his body relax. And I knew he was home.

A PERSON OF INTEREST

ERNEST HILL

ABOUT THIS GUIDE

The suggested questions are intended to
enhance your group's reading
of this book.

DISCUSSION QUESTIONS

1. What is the central theme of the story?

2. Compare and contrast the relationship that Luther and Felicia had with their respective spouses. In what ways did their marital relationships impact their ability to cope with their past and their future?

3. Felicia and her mother have varying views of Luther. How would you characterize Luther? Is he an honorable man or does he have character flaws that would deem him an unsavory person? Explain.

4. Olivia, Daphne, and Hattie are pivotal characters. What are your perceptions of them? How does their presence influence the plot?

5. Juanita was suspicious of Luther's faithfulness. Was she justified in her feelings? Or was she becoming an overbearing wife? Explain.

6. Do you feel that Luther's arrest constituted exemplary police work or a rush to judgment? Explain.

7. On several different occasions Luther was haunted by demons. What did the demons represent? How did they affect his behavior? What did they reveal about him? How were others influenced by those encounters?

8. Explain the significance of the initial meeting between Felicia and Joshua Edwards. What impact, if any, did it have on the resolution of the story?

9. At what point does Luther realize the need to take control of his impending demise? What was his motivation?

10. Are any of the characters self-serving? Explain.

11. Was Luther aware of Felicia's constant love? If so, does he react in any specific ways to illustrate his feelings?

12. There are several societal issues depicted throughout the story. Discuss the implication of each as it relates to the plot. In particular, discuss suicide, gambling, dissolutions of relationships, mental illness, love and serving as a caregiver for elderly parents.

13. Does the ending of the story provide closure for everyone? If so, explain.

14. By the conclusion of the novel do you believe that Luther's life has been redeemed? If so, how?